W9-AOT-738

THE SUMMER OF
THE GREAT DIVIDE

THE SUMMER OF THE GREAT DIVIDE

Linda Oatman High

Holiday House/New York

Library of Congress Cataloging-in-Publication Data
High, Linda Oatman.
The summer of the great divide / Linda Oatman High.—1st ed.
p.   cm.
Summary: Thirteen-year-old Wheezie spends the summer on a farm
where she deals with her learning-disabled cousin, her uncle's death
in Vietnam, and her parents' impending divorce.
ISBN 0-8234-1228-8 (alk. paper)
[1. Divorce—Fiction.   2. Cousins—Fiction.   Farm life—
Fiction.]   I. Title.
PZ7.H543968Su   1996   95-33532   CIP   AC
[Fic]—dc20

FOR ALL THE PARENTS:
Dad and Annette
Mom and Brad
Mom and Dad High

WITH THANKS TO:

Ray Fegley, for farm advice

Karen Nescot, for TV help

The Dreamcatchers Writers Group, for listening to the chicken chapter while eating pizza at Zia Maria's

Margery Cuyler, for editorial horse sense

John High, for taking the kids Somewhere Close, but Far Enough, when I needed time to write

All who served in Vietnam, those who came home, and those who didn't

Contents

THE SUMMER OF
THE GREAT DIVIDE

Chapter One

Going in All Different Directions

It was the thick of July 1969, and scorching sunlight blazed straight through the open car window and onto my arm.

"Holy moley," I muttered, staring at the backs of my parents' heads, so still and serious. Ever since we left home, Mama and Daddy had been quiet as two storm clouds brooding side by side in the sky. Wouldn't you know they'd pick the hottest day of the summer to dump me off?

Mama turned, craning to look at me. "What's the problem, Wheezie?" she asked.

I rolled my eyes, scowling. *What's the problem? The problem is that I'm being ditched half-*

3

way across the state while you two try to make up your minds about a divorce. Dumped off in a place I don't want to be as you do something I don't want you to do.

"What's wrong?" Mama asked, and I sighed.

"Nothing," I said. *Everything*, I thought. *Stuck for the summer on a stupid farm with Uncle Ollie, Aunt Ida, and Slow Roscoe: the strangest relatives on earth.*

"I can't stand Slow Roscoe," I said to the back of Mama's head.

"Oh, Wheezie," Mama remarked, "give him a chance. Get to know him better. Maybe you'll like him by the end of the summer."

I snorted. I'd *never* like Slow Roscoe, the cousin who was in special ed at school and a special bed at home, crackling with plastic sheets on account of his bed-wetting problem. Roscoe was the same age as I was—going on thirteen—but he acted more like *three*.

"I hate farms," I declared. "They kill animals on farms."

"It'll do you good, Wheezie," Mama said, her voice floating from the front of her head.

"Fresh air, hard work, sunshine, exercise."

"I hate sunshine," I said, yanking my arm from the sunlight and into the shade. "I hate fresh air." I cranked up the window and crossed my arms, slumping down in the seat and staring at green trees whizzing past in a fast blur of countryside.

"I miss Jess," I said, changing the subject as I always did when a fight was brewing.

Daddy nodded. "I know you do, honey," he said, quiet and sad.

"Jess says that you two shouldn't get a divorce," I added, crossing my fingers. Jess didn't really say that, but I knew she would, if only they'd ask her. Divorce was a cussword, far as my best friend, Jess, was concerned. She was ripped apart by it eight years ago, torn in two by the same people who made her. Jess had to divide *everything* in half: her heart, her home, her clothes, her school papers, even her teeth . . . saving the top for her mother and the bottom for her father.

And now my parents were dividing *me:* ripping me apart, shipping me off for the summer, separating us the way the yellow lines on the highway divided two sides of the road. *The Summer of the Great Divide*, I thought, gazing at the gray seat rising like a vinyl wall between us, dividing *me* from *them*.

And something invisible was dividing *them*. Pulling like a pair of giant pliers, prying them apart and wedging a barrier of pain and anger and sadness between them. I wished with all my heart we could be a family, just as we *used* to be.

"Do you remember," I said, "how you two used to finish sentences for each other all the time? And how sometimes you'd say the exact same thing at the exact same time?"

"We don't do that anymore," Mama said.

Daddy didn't say anything, just stared at the gray road, yellow lines, and blue sky, then flicked on the radio. A man's voice filled the car, talking on and on about the war in Vietnam.

"We shouldn't be there in the first place," Mama commented. Daddy angrily switched off the radio, and a tense silence seeped into the car, searing as the sun. I stared at the copper band circling my wrist and traced the engraved letters: *OB, Obadiah Byler, MIA*

6/8/68. Mama and Uncle Ollie's younger brother, Ob, was missing in action, lost somewhere in the jungles of Vietnam. He'd been gone for more than a year.

"I wish Ob would come home from Vietnam," I said. "The farm was a lot more fun with Ob around."

"Ob shouldn't be in Vietnam," Mama said, her voice tight.

"Olivia," said Daddy, making Mama's name sound sour in his mouth. "Ob is serving his country. *My* country. *Your* country."

Mama didn't say anything. She closed her eyes and leaned her head against the window. Her mouth was in a tight line.

I sighed. If they couldn't agree about Vietnam—so far away—how would they ever agree about anything *here?*

"Could I get a mood ring like Jess has?" I asked, changing the subject again. *Wheezie Moore, Queen of the Subject Changers. Wheezie Moore, Child of Divorce.* I liked the first title better.

"We'll see about a mood ring, Wheezie," Mama replied in a tired voice. *We'll see* was Mama's favorite answer to questions she didn't want to answer. That's what she said whenever I asked about her and Daddy getting a divorce. *We'll see.*

The turn signal clicked, and Daddy turned right. Sunlight flooded my face, and I slid across the seat, rolling down the window.

"Grace, Pennsylvania," Daddy proclaimed, as if we were entering the gates of heaven or something. A tiny wooden road sign perched rickety in the ditch, stuck in the mud at the end of Cowpoke Road. "We're almost there."

"Do you have everything you need for the summer, Wheezie?" Mama asked, and I took a deep breath.

"We'll see," I said.

The car moved slowly down Cowpoke Road, veering around potholes and tractors and chickens and dogs. I stared through the windshield, seeing gray road, brown dirt, and black holes. "Bor-ing," I muttered. "Grace, Pennsylvania, is the most boring place on earth."

I moved to the middle of the seat, positioning myself so that I could see my face in the rearview mirror, just as I'd seen our home reflected when we'd left this morning. Daddy turned the car into the pebbly driveway of the farm, and I was jostled left and right as the tires climbed the steep drive.

I don't like Mama and I don't like Daddy, I thought, looking at the backs of their heads swaying like stray balloons on separate strings. *But I love them both.* The farm loomed ahead, ugly and big, as the smell of manure leaked sharp through the open windows.

"Here we are," Daddy said, stopping the car. There was a thick silence as we each sat lost in our own little world for a moment. And then Daddy turned, reached out, and took my hand. "This will be better . . ." he said.

"Than you think it will be," Mama finished, and I caught my breath, a spark of hope lifting my heart as we climbed from the car and looked around at the farm.

"We'll see," I said, as first Mama and then Daddy held me tight in a hug. We pulled apart, and each of us made our own separate way across the rocky drive, a family going in all different directions and none of us quite sure where we were heading.

Chapter Two

Queen of the Corn

"Wheezie!" hollered Aunt Ida, lumbering barefoot across the ramshackle front porch, a bushel basket cradled in her pudgy arms. "I swear, you're growin' like a weed!"

"Um . . . thanks," I stammered, not quite sure if being compared to a weed was a compliment or not.

"Skinny as a beanpole, though!" Aunt Ida pronounced, taking stock of my body with her hard marble eyes shining blue and cold behind black-rimmed glasses. "Why, you're nuthin' but skin and bones and nose, flat as an ironing board! Don't you fret, though. We'll have you fattened up by the end of the summer."

I looked down at my chest (or what *would* be my chest, maybe someday), then up at Aunt Ida, who was shaped as square as a stack of firewood.

"You can put your suitcase in Ob's room," she said, planting the bushel basket in a corner of the porch.

I nodded, making my way up the rotten steps and following Aunt Ida. The wood creaked and groaned as we walked in silence across the ancient porch.

"Roscoe's watchin' the television," remarked Aunt Ida, yanking open the screen door. "You know that boy and his shows."

"I know," I said. *I wish I didn't*, I thought.

Aunt Ida stomped across the linoleum kitchen floor, heading for the dark stairway that led upstairs. I paused, hearing the loud sounds of a game show blaring from the living room. This house was old, so old that every noise seemed to echo like a yell. I sighed, thinking of home: our nice new ranch house, with every room painted bright and fresh and shiny. Here, everything was so *stale*, like a loaf of moldy old bread that should have been thrown away years ago. Stale and dreary and faded, with a smell like spoiled fruit.

"Cuck-oo, cuck-oo!" hooted the clock as I passed, the tiny painted bird poking through its door and making me jump. *Only two o'clock*, I thought, trailing after Aunt Ida. Time on the farm always seemed as slow as molasses, a whole different kind of time from what we had at home.

Something slimy and wet slopped across my leg and I shrieked, leaping onto the first step.

"That's Buford," Aunt Ida said, trudging up the steps ahead. "Roscoe's new bluetick hound."

I looked down, and there was a dog as fat as a hog, spotted brown on splotchy-white and dirty. His ears were two flaps of black, dangling limp and long past a pointed face and slimy nose dotted with dust. Buford's eyes were mud-brown and gooey, oozing mucky stuff that clung to the corners like gunked tears. He was the ugliest dog I'd ever seen, and had a terrible smell that even a dog shouldn't have.

"Buford," I said, "you have bad breath." The dog looked up at me, wagged a stub of a tail, then passed gas.

"Gross," I said, climbing the steps. Aunt Ida was in Ob's room—*my* room—fiddling around with the curtains.

"You have the best view of the farm," she reported as I plunked my suitcase beside the wardrobe. This old house—which had once belonged to Granny and Gramps—didn't have closets, or an indoor toilet, or hot running water.

I went to the window and gazed out: falling-down outbuildings in shades of gray, rusted wire fences surrounding bobbing and clucking chickens, the big barn peeling with red paint like a bad sunburn, patches of grass and huge trees and fields of corn, stretching forever in rows and rows that reached high into the sky. I saw Mama, sitting in the shade beneath the grapevine, and Daddy, gabbing with Uncle Ollie up by the barn. From here my parents looked like little Fisher-Price toy people, the kind that came as part of the Family Farm. I wished Mama and Daddy really *were* toys; I'd place them together, side by side, and never move them apart. And I'd put *me* in the middle.

"Wheezie," Aunt Ida said in her hoarse voice, "after you're settled, your chore is to pick some corn for supper."

Chore! I'd been here only ten minutes, for heaven's sake. Aunt Ida had no respect for guests. I sighed and turned from the window, tagging along behind Aunt Ida and her wild red hair.

"Holy moley," I muttered to myself, "I hate it already."

"Hi, Cousin Wheezie." It was Slow Roscoe, looking just as slow as ever, with his pasty-white face and oily black hair. "Want to watch TV?"

"Can't," I snapped. "I have work to do."

"Fresh air, exercise, sunshine," I recited as I stomped outside into the sweltering heat. "Work, work, work. Boring, boring, boring."

I snatched the bushel basket from the porch and headed for the corn, seeing Uncle Ollie's blue bib overalls from the corner of my eye.

"Greetings, Wheezie," he called in his raspy voice. "Welcome to Grace."

"Um . . . thanks," I said, squinting against the sun. I was sweating like a stuck pig, dripping and drenched.

"Where are you off to, honey?" Daddy yelled.

"To the corn," I replied, entering the kingdom of the corn. *Wheezie Moore, Queen of the Corn.* I bowed down to my subjects, getting my knees all dirty, and began to pluck the ripe ears of Silver Queen from the stalks, tossing them into the basket. "I . . . hate . . . farms," I chanted with each rip of the corn. "I . . . hate . . . divorce."

And then I, Wheezie Moore, Queen of the Corn, decreed an order never to be broken in the land of make-believe. "No more divorce forevermore," I ruled, waving my wand of corn. "All parents will stay together forever, for always and a day, until death do them part."

But this was real life, and I could see through the cornstalks that Mama and Daddy were standing on either side of the car, getting ready to leave me behind.

And that's when Wheezie Moore, Queen of the Corn, changed into Wheezie Moore, Child of Divorce. I started to cry, making my way through the maze to tell my parents good-bye.

Chapter Three

The Slaughter of the Chickens

Heat lay heavy upon my head, choking my throat and making my heart ache as I waited on a stump for Uncle Ollie to fetch the ax.

"Wheezie Moore," hollered Slow Roscoe, from somewhere in the middle of the corn crop, "come on down! You're the next contestant . . . on . . . 'THE PRICE IS RIGHT'!"

I sighed, holding my head in my hands. Roscoe was like a stuck record, saying the same stupid words over and over, trying to sound just like the announcer on his favorite game show. That was all Slow Roscoe ever did: gawk at television and holler. I was beginning to despise him more and more every minute, and it was only my second day on the farm.

He was calling me again, this time from behind the outhouse. "Wheezie Moore," he shouted, "come on down!"

"Stifle, Roscoe," I muttered. "Shut up." Uncle Ollie was on his way, limping across the overgrown yard with the ax clutched close to his chest, glinting silver in the sunlight. The Chicken-Killing Ax, which was usually stuck into a rotting beam on the log ceiling of the outkitchen.

Tossing down the ax, Uncle Ollie made his lopsided way into the midst of the chickens, whistling a hymn as he gimped along and kicked at Mister Cocky, the boot-pecking, red-necked rooster.

Slow Roscoe stumbled into sight, dumb Buford waddling behind. For the life of me, I couldn't figure out which one was more stupid: Roscoe or Buford.

"I got the cwothes hanger, Pap," hollered Roscoe, poking me with his bony elbow as he passed by. "You's gonna wike this, Wheezie," he said. Slow Roscoe had a speech impediment and just couldn't get his buck-teeth and blubbery tongue in the right position for the *L* sound. Actually, it was Roscoe who started calling me Wheezie instead of Louise, back when he was still in diapers. Shoot, for all I knew, Slow Roscoe was *still* in diapers.

Roscoe stretched a metal coat hanger high above his head, looking as if he thought he could hook the sky, if he tried. "Chickens are *so* funny without their heads," he said to me.

My stomach churned. Roscoe made me sick, with his eyes all lit up and shining, so excited about the killing to come. As I watched, Roscoe twisted and bent the metal of the hanger into a chicken-catching stick with a hook on the end. Mama told me all about those, in her never-ending stories of Life on the Farm.

Roscoe presented the hanger to Uncle Ollie, who peered down at the cluster of chickens at his feet. They were clucking and pecking like there was no tomorrow, bobbing their heads and scratching in the dirt.

Uncle Ollie looked at the chickens, looked at the hook, and then in the fastest movement I ever saw him make, latched on to the leg of one of the chickens: The White Giant, with feathers like snow and eyes as black as night. He snatched it up, clenching its dark yellow claws tight in his hand, then turned it upside down.

"Got her!" Slow Roscoe hollered. Buford barked, running circles around Uncle Ollie as he carried the fat white chicken to the stump, with Roscoe right behind him.

"This'll make a fine pot of chicken stew," Uncle Ollie said to nobody in particular. "More meat on this girl than sunshine in the sky."

I covered my eyes, thinking of how Mama had insisted that a summer on her brother's farm would do me good. I wasn't feeling so good now, with the sound of the White Giant's last squawks echoing in my mind.

"All right, Roscoe," said Uncle Ollie in his kind and gentle rasp of a voice, "line up her head."

The White Giant clucked and blinked a coal-black eye, as Uncle Ollie bent to pick up the ax.

I couldn't look away, no matter how hard

I tried. My insides didn't want to watch, but my eyes were tied to the chicken, the ax, and Uncle Ollie.

Uncle Ollie squinted, the chicken clucked, and the ax swung, a sharp flash of fast silver.

Uncle Ollie tossed the body into the green grass, and it flipped and jumped in a crazy, headless dance.

It seemed like forever, Buford barking and chasing the chicken body as it hopped.

I took a deep breath, dizzy at the sight of white feathers, black eyes, blue sky, red blood, and green grass.

Then I threw up.

Chapter Four

The Vietnam War Show

Aunt Ida was plucking the White Giant, steam and stink rising from the kettle as she yanked on the feathers, dropping them like snow into the sink.

"Pay attention, Wheezie," she said. "We promised your mama to teach you a few things about livin' off the earth." That was one of Aunt Ida's favorite sayings: "Livin' off the earth." That, and "make do with what you have."

Slumping down on the kitchen chair and unsticking my thighs from the red vinyl, I sighed. "I hate livin' off the earth," I said. "The slaughter of the chickens makes me sick."

Aunt Ida snorted. "Wheezie, you ain't seen nuthin' yet. Wait until fall, when we butcher for the winter freezer." She jabbed at her glasses, leaving a tiny spike of white fluff on the shiny black rim.

My stomach was flipping faster than the beheaded chicken. I took a slow sip of the ginger ale Aunt Ida forced on me, fizzing away cool and sweet in a Snoopy-dog jelly glass.

"Fall?" I said, more a breath than a question. "I'll be going home before fall."

Aunt Ida turned to look at me, all flush-faced from steam, her wiry hair frizzy like unraveled rope.

"Wheezie," she said, "your mama called to talk to me while you were out back."

I caught my breath.

Aunt Ida's glasses fogged, and she whipped them off and wiped them on the tail of her shirt. "She said that maybe it would be best if you'd just stay a spell, until everything is worked out and divvied up and such." Aunt Ida's eyes, blue-speckled and hard, were as empty of expression as the ice cubes clinking cold against my teeth.

I chewed fiercely on a chunk of ice, swallowing and searching Aunt Ida's face for something she might have been hiding inside. Something she knew, but I didn't.

"Are they getting a divorce, for sure?" I asked, staring at the red-and-white-checked oilcloth until it blurred.

Aunt Ida shrugged, adjusting her glasses on her beak of a nose. "Who knows?" she said, shifting back to the chicken. "Only the good Lord and the lawyers." She snorted, plucking close around the neck of the bird.

I swallowed, smelling the awful odor of wet feathers and just-killed chicken. I could hear Slow Roscoe in the living room, talking a blue streak to the television screen.

"I guess I'll go watch television," I said, carefully placing the jelly glass on the table. "I'm not feeling very good."

Aunt Ida nodded, and I made my way into the dark little living room, my head spinning. Roscoe was perched on the couch, scrunching one of Aunt Ida's fancy doilies in his hands.

"These people drive me crazy," he said, gritting his buckteeth and coiling the doily around his dirty fingers. "If *I* could be on this show, you could bet your sweet bippy I'd come home with wots of prizes."

"Roscoe," I said, flopping down beside him, "what would you do if your parents were getting a divorce?"

Roscoe looked at me, eyes bulging and mouth open, not a pretty sight with that bread-dough face of his. He gaped at me, then turned back to the TV.

"Not the Vietnam War again," he whined, as a news flash shot across the screen. "I hate that show."

"The Vietnam War isn't a show, stupid," I said, rolling my eyes. "It's real life . . . and death."

I touched the band on my wrist and closed my eyes, remembering Ob two Christmases ago, holding high the redbird feather I gave him. Eyes shining blue like sky, Uncle Ob flashed me a smile and then read the card: "Dear Ob: This feather is for good luck in the Vietnam War. It's from a redbird who flew from the tree you planted for me when I was born. Use it to fly away from Vietnam and back home again, when the war gets too bad to stand. Love, Your Niece Wheezie."

"I'll keep it for always, Wheezie," Ob said, sticking the feather in his pocket, above his heart. Two weeks later, he flew off to Vietnam. And where was he now? Shaking off the thought, I opened my eyes.

"Roscoe," I said, "how can you stand all the killing around here? All the blood, and the guts, and the stink, and the feathers, and the mess?"

Roscoe shrugged, his scrawny shoulders brushing the bottoms of his jug ears. Roscoe had the biggest ears I ever saw, all filled up with the sounds of that black-and-white TV he worshiped from morning till night.

"The slaughter of the chickens was sick," I pronounced.

"Wheezie," said Roscoe, laughing in his strange way: *hiss, gasp, snuffle. Hiss, gasp, snuffle.* When something really tickled Slow Roscoe's funny bone, he sounded something akin to a pig at the trough.

Hiss, gasp, snuffle. Roscoe went on and on, practically rolling on the floor over some private joke.

"What on earth is so all-fired funny?" I asked.

"The swaughter of the chickens," Slow Roscoe tittered. "You onwy saw *one* chicken die, Wheezie."

"Roscoe," I said, "when one chicken is killed, it affects all the others, in one way or another. It's just like the Vietnam War: one guy dies and it hurts everybody. We all die."

"Let's change the channel," said Slow Roscoe. "I hate the Vietnam War Show."

It was then that I heard it: a low, sad wail, like a baby's cry, coming from smack-dab in the center of my chest.

Chapter Five

The Barn Owl

Slouched on the front steps and staring at Cowpoke Road, I bided my time hacking and coughing, waiting for some boondocks doctor Aunt Ida claimed made house calls.

The low moan inside of me had turned into a full-blown wheeze, just like the time I had pneumonia and couldn't get a deep breath to save my life.

"Hey, Wheezie." It was Slow Roscoe, nose squashed against the screen door with a green ice pop clutched in his hand. "Want a Popsicle?"

I shook my head, gasping.

The door hinges squealed, and Roscoe

towered tall and scrawny above me, dribbling sticky green down his chin and onto his fingers.

"It's awmost time for 'The Beverwy Hiwbiwwies,'" said Roscoe, pulling the *TV Guide* from under his arm. "Want to come in and watch, Wheezie?"

"Why would I want to *watch* a bunch of hillbillies," I said, in between gasps and coughs, "when I'm *living* with some?"

Slow Roscoe shrugged and ambled off, sticking the *TV Guide* back in his armpit. Far as I knew, Roscoe couldn't even read a comic book, but he toted that glossy little *TV Guide* around as if it were his own personal bible or something. I figured he most likely just looked at the pictures and memorized the times of his shows, making believe that he was reading.

From the kitchen behind me, I could hear Slow Roscoe bleating the theme song from "The Beverly Hillbillies." Roscoe's singing was not a pretty sound, especially when he did it at the top of his lungs in that off-key, showoff way of his. I covered my ears, trying to block Roscoe out and wishing that the boondocks slowpoke doctor would get a move on and make tracks up Cowpoke Road, before my breath left me altogether. The wheezing was worse; now it sounded like a whole roomful of babies crying from somewhere in the middle of my chest, with my heart racing to get the heck out of that mess.

You cursed me, Roscoe, I thought. *You cursed me with that stupid name: Wheezie.*

And now the name fit. *Wheezie.* My breathing sounded just about as bad as Roscoe's laugh. *Hiss, gasp, snuffle. Hiss, gasp, snuffle. Hiss, gasp, snuffle, cough, wheeze.*

"How are you doin', Wheezie?" It was Aunt Ida, standing at the screen door, that chicken feather still stuck to her glasses and sweat beading her upper lip.

"Call me Louise," I gasped.

"What?" asked Aunt Ida.

"Never mind," I said, and went back to the business of trying to breathe. Funny how you take something like breathing for granted until it's so hard to do.

"Sounds like you might've caught hold of some ragweed allergy," Aunt Ida said. "Ollie gets that every summer, round about this time. Makes a soul cough and wheeze and sneeze, carryin' on just like you are now. Why, I never in all my born days heard such racket as comes from Ollie's nose and throat in July."

I nodded and bowed my head, just wanting her to go away and be quiet. I wanted my mama . . . or my daddy . . . or both of them, together. That would be best: all of us *together*, the way a family should be.

There was a rattle and a roar, then a spew of stones in the driveway. I peered through the dust and saw an old truck eaten up by rust, with a red tailgate and blue fenders and a cab the color of calf poop.

"Dr. Mack," pronounced Aunt Ida.

"Holy moley," I whispered.

The driver's door creaked open and out climbed some old guy with a face like a barn owl, toting a big black bag. "That's the doctor?" I whispered.

"That's the doctor," said Aunt Ida, pushing up her glasses. "Best doctor in these parts, too."

Probably the only doctor in these parts, I thought, watching The Barn Owl lumber across the yard. He walked as if he had bowel problems. *The Barn Owl with a Bad Bowel.* I almost laughed, in between wheezes.

"Hello, Miss Ida," said The Barn Owl, heaving himself and his bag up the steps and onto the porch. He was wheezing, too, breathing heavy and loud like an overworked plow horse. *Great*, I thought, *the doctor is sicker than I am.*

"Hello, young lady," The Barn Owl huffed, unzipping the bag and sticking a stethoscope into his hairy ears, then sliding the cold end down my chest.

"Wheezie," said Aunt Ida.

"Sure is," said The Barn Owl, nodding.

"I mean that's her name," said Aunt Ida. "Wheezie. Short for Louise. Our niece."

The Barn Owl nodded again, beady black eyes almost crossing as he got a load of my breathing. He listened to my chest, then my back, then my heart, then my chest again.

"Asthma," he said, those deep-set eyes almost disappearing in his fat face.

"What?" I asked.

"Asthma," said The Barn Owl, whipping the stethoscope out of his ears and tossing it into his bag. "Allergic condition, marked by coughing, wheezing, and difficulty in breathing."

"So what do I do?" I asked, as Mister Know-It-All Barn Owl rummaged in that messy black bag of his.

"I was getting to that, miss," he said, yanking out a little bottle with a plastic piece on the end. "Shake, put this in the mouth, exhale, inhale, hold breath, exhale. Easy as pie."

He handed the bottle to me, and I shook it, then stuck the plastic end in my mouth. *Exhale, inhale, hold breath, exhale.* It was magic: the wheezing stopped, the coughing stopped, I could breathe.

"Told you he was the best doctor in these parts," said Aunt Ida. "This man could cure a ham."

The Barn Owl zipped up his bag, winked a black eye, and flew away, flapping his wings and heading for his truck of rust. A rattle, a roar, a spew of stones, and he was gone, leaving Aunt Ida and me behind, chasing dust from our eyes.

Buford barked and Uncle Ollie coughed

from somewhere in the darkness of the barn.

"Well," said Aunt Ida, "back to my chicken stew."

I took a deep breath, smelling truck exhaust and lilacs and something cooking in the kitchen.

"Wheezie Moore," hollered Slow Roscoe from the living room, "come on down! You're the next contestant."

"Stifle, Roscoe," I whispered, as Aunt Ida bustled back to the kitchen, and I wished with all my heart to go home.

Chapter Six

Together Forever

I was in my bedroom—*Ob*'s bedroom—huddled in the corner where the telephone hung on the wall. There was more privacy in this room than anywhere else in the house.

Lifting the black receiver and pressing it to my ear, I dialed home.

"Mama?" I said when she answered. "I have asthma. I think I should come home."

"What?" asked Mama's voice, floating from faraway across those telephone wires stretched from home to Grace.

"I said I HAVE ASTHMA!" I shouted.

"Oh," said Mama. "Asthma, you say?"

"Yes," I whispered, almost ready to cry. I

35

wasn't sure why, but tears burned my eyes like fire as I stared at the blue-flowered wallpaper blooming all over the room.

"I had asthma every summer when I lived there," announced Mama, as if proclaiming the fact that her eyes had always been brown. "It's all that ragweed pollen hanging in the air."

I brushed my hair from my eyes, blinking hard. "That's what Aunt Ida says. The doctor gave me an inhaler to use." There was a click, and I knew that somebody was listening in on the party line. Aunt Ida and Uncle Ollie had three neighbors who shared their telephone line, and they were as nosy as all-get-out.

"And, Mama," I said, real loud, "Aunt Ida likes to run around outside at nighttime, wearing only her undies." There was a breath, then a click.

"She does?" asked Mama, laughing.

"Not really," I said. "Somebody was on the party line again. Nosy old Evie Nettle, most likely. That woman has nothing better to do than listen to everybody else's conversations all day long, Aunt Ida says. She says if you shock her enough, she'll hang up."

"Well, Aunt Ida in her skivvies would be enough to shock anybody," Mama said, and I snickered.

"So," I said, taking a deep breath, "are you and Daddy getting a divorce?" I crossed my fingers, my feet, and my eyes.

"Oh, Wheezie, I don't know," Mama said. "I'm so mixed up lately that I don't know what I do know. That's why you're better off staying there on the farm until things are settled."

"I hate the farm," I muttered.

Mama laughed. "Nobody could hate the farm, Wheezie," she said. "Living off the earth, making do with what you have, getting lots of fresh air and sunshine and exercise. You're just feeling moody again, aren't you?"

I sighed. "I have more moods than this farm has manure, Mama," I said. "My spirits go up and down and in and out, like the rising and setting of the sun, and I can't change how I feel any more than I can change the sunshine. What's wrong with me?"

"You're growing up, Wheezie," said

Mama, "and there's nothing wrong with that."

Those words kept playing through my mind, again and again, after we said our good-byes and I hung up the phone. *You're growing up, Wheezie, and there's nothing wrong with that.* If I was growing up, then why did I feel like such a baby?

Flopping down on the creaky bed, I looked around the room—Ob's room, and Mama's before that. Mama and Ollie and Ob were born in this house, along with the little girl baby who died of whooping cough in my granny's arms so many years ago. And now Granny and Gramps were gone, too, leaving only this house, the farm, and all of us. I wondered what my grandparents would think of Mama and Daddy getting a divorce.

"They shouldn't do it, should they?" I asked the big picture hanging over the bed. "They shouldn't divide our family, tear me in two, mess everything up. It's 'till death do us part,' right?" Granny and Gramps stared back at me, wire-framed glasses and gray hair glinting in the flash of the camera.

"I know you two never would have gotten

a divorce," I said to the gold-framed photograph. "Why, just look at you: you're two peas in a pod. That's how Mama and Daddy should be." Granny and Gramps, together forever on a background of blue, didn't answer. Just stared, from somewhere in time, at their only granddaughter.

"If Mama and Daddy get a divorce," I told the picture, "they may as well cut out my heart and chop it in two: one for him and one for her. And then there's nothing left for *me*, because there's not enough of me to go around."

I stood and looked into the mirror above the bureau, a wrinkled wavy oval of old glass. Brown hair, brown eyes, big nose, sad mouth. I pushed my hair from my eyes and stuck out my tongue, wishing that mirrors could lie. There was a new crop of zits, sprouting anew from my chin.

"If you two saw me now," I said, turning back to the big photograph of Granny and Gramps, "would you know it was me? Would you recognize me, now that I'm growing up?"

And then, in a flash of time that I couldn't

have stopped if I tried, the picture of Granny and Gramps fell fast from the wall and onto the floor, crashing into jagged splinters of glass. I caught my breath and took a step, looking up at the dark square of wallpaper where the picture had hung, then down at the zillions of glass fragments on the floor. I reached out and plucked the photograph from the smashed glass, holding it carefully by the corners.

They were still there: Granny and Gramps, together forever, frozen in time and fallen from the wall where they used to live. I took a deep breath and held them to my chest, making my way across the sharp glass.

"Wheezie!" came Aunt Ida's voice through the grate in the floor that was supposed to allow winter heat to seep from the coal stove below, up into the bedrooms. "Wheezie, it's time to eat."

"Wheezie Moore!" hollered Slow Roscoe, and I could see his upturned face through the hole, peering from the living room. "Come on down! You're the next contestant on . . . 'THE PRICE IS RIGHT'!"

"Stifle, Roscoe," I sighed, then covered

the hole with Granny and Gramps, who now stared straight up at the water spot on the ceiling.

"See what I have to put up with," I whispered to my grandparents, and then I headed downstairs for supper.

Chapter Seven

Human Beings Hightailing It to the Moon

Aunt Ida was crocheting in the rocking chair, Uncle Ollie was snoring on the sofa, and Roscoe and I were sprawled on the floor, waiting in the TV-lit room for men to walk on the moon.

"They sure do make it look real, don't they?" Aunt Ida said, looking up from the yarn twisted through her fingers. The hooked needle fell still in her hands, as she and Roscoe and I gazed at the television screen. "I swear, that Apollo Eleven looks like it could zoom right into our living room."

I slid a sideways glance at Roscoe, who gawked at the space machine on the screen, his mouth open and eyes wide. Flopping over onto my back, I looked up through the window at the moon, hung low and lazy like a paste-faced clown over the corn. It was hard to imagine: human beings hightailing it to the moon at that very moment.

Rain began to splatter across the tin roof and a rumble of thunder shook the room, making Uncle Ollie's eyes fly open and his mouth clamp closed. "It's that space machine," he said, stretching, "messin' up our weather by flyin' so high."

Aunt Ida tightened her lips and shook her head, going back to crocheting the sweater or blanket or whatever she was working on with that needle and yarn.

I yawned, wondering if Mama and Daddy were watching the space journey, together or apart. If I was home, we'd all watch *together*, that was for sure.

"Beam me up, Scottie," said Roscoe, imitating his favorite space show, "Star Trek." Uncle Ollie laughed, and Buford wagged his stub tail back and forth like a flag. Roscoe claimed that a coyote chewed off the rest of Buford's tail, but anybody in his or her right mind knew that there was no such thing as coyotes in Grace, Pennsylvania.

"If *I* was on that space machine," said Slow Roscoe, "I'd almost pee my pants from excitement."

"You pee your pants every night," I muttered, and Roscoe nudged me with his bony elbow.

"Shut up," he said. "Stifle."

I turned away and watched the moon through the window, thinking how the same moon hung over home, and Hollywood, and Uncle Ob in Vietnam. It was hard to believe, somehow, that one moon could serve the whole world, lighting up the night for all different kinds of people.

As I listened to the sound of rain skittering and Buford panting and Roscoe breathing all snortylike through his mouth, a cow mooed from the barn, and crickets chirped outside.

"Do you know," said Uncle Ollie, "that crickets can tell the temperature within two degrees? All you have to do is count the number of chirps in fourteen seconds, add forty, and you have the temperature."

I looked at Uncle Ollie, while the words

"the *Eagle* has landed" floated from the TV and into the dark living room. Uncle Ollie sat up straight, Aunt Ida stopped crocheting, and Slow Roscoe's smile faded from his face. My heart rose into my throat like a rocket into the sky, and I stared.

An astronaut in a white and bulky space suit climbed from the spiderlike machine, down onto the ladder leading to the moon. The Sea of Tranquillity.

"I'm going to step off now," came the voice. "That's one small step for a man, one giant leap for mankind."

"And womankind," I whispered.

"The surface is fine and powdery," said the television voice. "It sticks in fine layers like powdered charcoal to the soles and sides of my boots."

"What if the whole moon crumbles and falls to earth?" asked Aunt Ida, forgetting that she didn't believe in moonwalkers.

"We can send men to the moon, but we can't feed the hungry in America," said Uncle Ollie.

"Sssshhh!" said Slow Roscoe, and everybody was quiet.

The second astronaut came down the steps, and the two men fetched rocks and hopped around as if they were on the carnival moonwalk ride down at the Grace County Annual Fair.

"They look more like toys than men," I said, watching them jump up and down, up and down.

Then one of the men planted the flag—the same flag I pledged to in school—and gave it the grandest salute I ever saw in all my born days.

"Here men from the planet Earth first set foot upon the moon. July 1969. We came in peace for all mankind."

The words burned tears down my cheeks, and the room was silent. Even Buford was as still as the stars, snuggled up on the floor at my feet. It was a moment I knew I'd remember forever, for all my time on earth.

We watched for a while, listening to the president talk about peace and hope, as I looked at the huge moon and thought how it was closer than ever before.

"I'm going to bed," I said. "Earth people need their sleep."

Trudging up the steps, I heard Slow Roscoe behind me. "I'm going to do that someday," he said. "Wawk on the moon."

"That'll be the day, Roscoe," I said, heading into the night. "That'll be the day."

Chapter Eight

The Eagle *Has Wanded*

"The *Eagle* has wanded!"

Slow Roscoe swung like a monkey from a branch of the oak tree that hung over Cowpoke Road, his feet dangling on the windshield of Evie Nettle's old mail Jeep. "The *Eagle* has wanded!" he hollered again, as Evie leaned out and shoved a handful of envelopes into the mailbox.

"More like an old bat than an eagle," I muttered, watching Evie sputter and putt down the road in that red, white, and blue Jeep full of other people's business. I figured that was why Evie delivered mail: to poke her nose into other people's private lives.

"Hey, Wheezie," yelled Roscoe from the road, "there's a fat package for you."

I put down the kettle of peas I was shelling and headed for the mailbox. "From Mama," I said, taking the big envelope from Roscoe's grubby hand.

Sauntering back to my seat beneath the grapevine, I waited until Roscoe went inside. Then I ripped open the package.

"Peace," I whispered, seeing a tie-dyed T-shirt decorated with a peace symbol and a dove. Mama was big on peace, ever since her baby brother Ob went to Vietnam instead of on his senior class trip. I touched the copper band on my wrist and gazed at the swirled colors on the shirt: twirls of pink and blue circling the symbol of peace.

Lifting out the shirt, I shook it, and something fell from the sleeve: a Bee-Beautiful Bra, with an embroidered bumblebee buzzing in the center.

"Mama," I said out loud, laughing. Mama always teased me that I had bee stings instead of breasts, and I could just imagine her thinking this was the biggest joke ever.

There was a note, folded and bulky, with

something inside. I flipped it open and saw a mood ring, with a band of gold and an oval stone black and shiny, just like the one Jess got for Christmas at her father's house. The note said:

Dearest Wheezie,

Peace. I bought you a T-shirt at an anti-war demonstration in Washington. It was a toss-up between the shirt and a poster. I decided on the shirt because it was something you could hold and keep forever. The words on the poster you can hold forever, too, in your heart. Here they are: "If you are yourself at peace, then there is at least some peace in the world. Share your peace with everyone and everyone will be at peace." Keep those words forever, Wheezie, and I won't have to buy the poster.

Hope you like the Bee-Beautiful. I'm sure you get the joke!

The mood ring was on sale at Sears, and I know how you've been wanting one. Since your moods are so change-able, I thought now would be a good

time to buy the ring! (It'll be very col-
orful.) It'll be black when you're not
wearing it, or when you're in a very bad
mood. Green means the best mood ever,
blue means sad, orange means confused,
red means angry, and pink means that
you're in love! (Hope it never turns pink
this summer!)

Wishing you lots of fun on the farm
. . . see you soon.

Love, Mama

Not a word about divorce, not a clue. I
stared at Mama's curvy handwriting, hoping
to find a hint hidden somewhere within her
big squiggly letters. It was signed just
Mama, no Daddy anywhere in sight. I wondered if it was that way in Mama's life, too.

"Hey, Wheezie, what'd you get?" It was
Slow Roscoe, and I shoved the bra inside the
shirt, hiding it from Roscoe's prying eyes.

"A shirt," I said. "And a ring. A mood
ring."

"A *moon* ring!" shouted Roscoe. "The *Ea-*

gle has wanded!" That was Roscoe's newest annoying saying, ever since the night of the moon walk.

"Not a *moon* ring," I said. "A *mood* ring. Tells my mood by its color."

Hiss, gasp, snuffle. Hiss, gasp, snuffle. "Wheezie," snorted Roscoe, "you don't need a ring to tell your mood. Just use your face." *Hiss, gasp, snuffle.* "Your *mood* face."

I rolled my eyes, slipping the ring onto the third finger of my left hand. Jess said that finger was kind of attached to the heart.

Watching the ring in the crisscross shade of the grapevine, I stared as the black slowly bled red. *Angry* red.

"Roscoe," I said, "isn't it time to go inside and watch 'Mister Ed'?" I wanted to see if I could make the ring turn green, but there was no chance of that with Slow Roscoe anywhere within spitting distance.

Roscoe peeled the *TV Guide* from his sweaty armpit. I swear, that must have been the worst-smelling *TV Guide* in Grace, Pennsylvania . . . maybe in the whole *world*.

"Nope," said Roscoe, thumbing through the pages. "Not time yet."

"Well, how about 'Lassie' or 'The Price Is Right' or 'The Beverly Hillbillies'?" The ring was as red as ripe tomatoes.

"Nope," said Roscoe, plucking a grape from the vine and squirting the insides into his mouth. "Just Ma's soap operas." He chewed the grape—*squish, squish, swallow*—then flicked the purple skin into the garden. A bunch of chickens came running, pecking and fighting for the peel. Roscoe grinned.

"Watch this," he said, and spit in the dust by the side of the garden. In a flock of feathers and bobbing heads, the gang of chickens rushed for the spot where the spit landed.

"They think it's something to eat," Roscoe tittered. "Chickens are *so* funny."

I rolled my eyes, furiously shelling peas into the kettle. The ring flashed red, shining bright over the pile of glossy green peas.

"Ma says we're having the last of Bacon Lady for supper tonight," Roscoe informed me. Actually, he said *Bacon Wady*.

I looked at Roscoe, frowning. "What on earth is Bacon Wady?" I asked.

"Pig," pronounced Roscoe, running a

hand through his greasy hair. "Ham." He licked his lips. "Yum-yum."

"Yuck," I said. "I'm having peas." I'd decided not to eat anything that used to walk.

Buford waddled across the yard and sniffed at the peace shirt in the grass.

"Buford," I said, "if you pee on that shirt, you're dead meat. Like everything else on this farm."

Roscoe gawked at me, dull blue eyes swelling with tears. "Wheezie," he said, "why are you so mean?"

I ignored him, shelling away at the peas.

"You hate Buford," declared Roscoe. "You hate our house, you hate our farm, you hate me. Maybe you even hate *you*." He stared at me, accusations slobbering across his dribbling lips.

"Why are you so mean?" he asked again.

"Roscoe," I said, staring into the kettle on my lap, "I don't mean to be mean. I just can't seem to help it lately. I'd like to see how *you* would act if *your* parents were getting a divorce."

Roscoe bit his lip, thinking. "I'd still be me," he said. "I wouldn't be mean."

I didn't answer him, just twisted the mood

ring around and around, staring at the oval of red.

"Come on, Wassie," Roscoe said to Buford, smacking his fat lips and patting his bony knee. Buford wobbled across the yard, tongue hanging out and stub wiggling.

Roscoe looked at me, his big ears red and backlighted by the sun. "I decided to call Buford Wassie," he said, "because he's so smart. Just like that famous dog on TV.

"The *Eagle* has wanded!" Roscoe yelled. Then he and Buford moseyed off across the yard: two dummies on their way to nowhere.

I sighed and stood, feeling cross and grouchy. "Lambchop," I mumbled, plopping the kettle of shelled peas into the grass. "Lambchop will cheer me up." Lambchop was my favorite animal on the entire farm, with her warm brown eyes and fuzzy white wool.

I headed for the barn, griping and grumbling all the way. Slow Roscoe drove me crazy, and so did stupid Buford. Even Uncle Ollie and Aunt Ida worked on my nerves, blabbing on and on about the weather as if their lives depended on it or something. I swear, these relatives had more ways of predicting rain than they had brains: pigs scratching their backsides on the fence posts, cows swishing their tails, Buford sniffing the air, the silver maple turning silver, daisies closing blossoms, a pale sun, a red moon, buttermilk sky, a ring of clouds way up high. The pigs were scratching their backsides now, I noticed, and the sky was growing darker by the minute, just like my mood.

Flinging open the barn door, I marched inside, inhaling the smell of cool hay and warm animals. "Lambchop," I called, "it's Wheezie." At least *Lambchop* wouldn't ask me why I was so mean, or accuse me of hating her.

A bleat sounded soft and low from Lambchop's stall, and I peered inside, pressing my face against the wooden slats. "Hi, Lambchop," I said. "I need some cheering up."

Lambchop smiled, sheepish and silly, from beneath her wild mop of wool. She reminded me of my fifth-grade teacher, Miss Lamberto, who had pure white hair and a frizzy perm that fell in her eyes. I smiled back.

"Miss Lambchop," I said, "you sure do know how to cheer me up."

Lambchop bleated and thunder rumbled, shaking the barn and my heart. "I'd better run inside before the storm hits," I told Lamb-chop. "Pigs were scratching their backsides, you know."

Taking a deep breath, I dashed outside, running down through the yard and snatch-ing up the peace shirt, my Bee-Beautiful, and the letter from Mama. Rain was begin-ning to fall, and I could hear Roscoe through the screen window, shouting at the TV.

"The *Eagle* has wanded," I muttered, mocking Slow Roscoe as I stomped up the porch steps and into the house.

"What did you say, Wheezie?" called Ros-coe as I trudged upstairs.

"Nothing," I said.

I padded into my room and switched on Ob's old radio. "I want to hold your hand," I sang along with the Beatles, crackling with static from the dusty brown speakers.

Rain pounded the tin roof, and I looked up, seeing the water spot spreading above my head. It was time for a bath, I decided, slipping out of my damp and dirty clothes and depositing them in a pile on the floor.

And then I saw it: drops of splotchy stuff in my underpants, red as the mood ring on my finger. Blood.

Chapter Nine

Uncle Harvey and My Other Strange Relatives

"Wheezie is a woman now," announced Aunt Ida. "Uncle Harvey came to visit."

I grimaced. *Uncle Harvey?* That was as bad as *The Curse* or *My Friend*, as girls in school said. I wrote a poem about all this nonsense last year for English class, titled "Uncle Harvey." It ran through my mind now, as Aunt Ida fussed around in her bedroom, producing all the stuff necessary to be a woman.

Uncle Harvey
is
here,
they say.

I've got My Friend,
The Curse,
It's That Time Again.
Guess
Who
Came
To
Visit?
Girls with The Curse,
always guessing,
when they know
full well
that it's only
Uncle Harvey
visiting
again,
My Friend.

I got an A for the poem, and it hung on the fridge for months, stuck there by Mama and a magnet.

"Aunt Ida," I said, "I need to call Mama."

Aunt Ida nodded. "Only problem is nosy old Evie Nettle. Why, all of Grace County will know Uncle Harvey came to visit."

I shrugged and headed for the telephone.

"Mama?" I said when she answered. "I got my period, finally." I sat on the bed, feeling fat and bulky and full of blood and stuff.

"Wonderful, honey!" Mama said, her voice loud and clear in my ear. "And did you get my package in the mail?"

"Yes," I said. "Thanks."

"You're a woman now, baby!" Mama raved, and there was a click. Evie Nettle. I could hear her breath.

"I feel more like a baby than ever," I said. "Wearing a diaper." There was a fast click, and I knew I'd shocked the old bat into hanging up.

"I think I should come home," I said. "And be a woman in my own house."

Mama laughed. "Oh, Wheezie," she said, "you are *so* funny." Now she sounded like Slow Roscoe.

I sighed, twisting the coils of the telephone cord around and around my hand. "Could I talk to Daddy?" I asked.

There was a pause, and then Mama's voice, quieter than before. "He's not here," she said. I caught my breath, releasing the coils from my hand.

"So," said Mama, perky and loud, "did you get that mood ring to turn green?"

I looked at the ring, orange as fire, then at my sad and pale face in the mirror across the room.

"Not yet, Mama," I said. "Probably won't be green until I'm home. Or maybe when you and Daddy decide not to get a divorce, or when Uncle Ob comes back from Vietnam."

I said good-bye and hung up the phone, alone with Uncle Harvey and Aunt Ida and my other strange relatives.

Chapter Ten

A Plan

"Did you know," said Slow Roscoe, "that the only part of the pig we waste is the squeawer?"

"The squealer?" I asked.

"The oink-oink box," said Slow Roscoe, pointing to his grimy throat. "The part that makes noise."

I shook my head, not really wanting to hear about it, but Slow Roscoe rambled on.

"We use the guts for sausage casing," he said. "We eat the feet, we eat the belly, we eat the whole head ground up in scrapple."

I covered my ears, humming, then plucked a blade of grass and used it as a whistle between my thumbs.

Slow Roscoe tried to do a cartwheel, flopping on his scrawny rear end with a thump. "The *Eagle* has wanded!" he hollered, then looked at me with a grin. "I'm fixing to walk on the moon someday," he said. "Me and Buford, the first boy and dog in outer space." He guffawed, and draped an arm around Buford.

"The first *moron* and dog in outer space," I said, chewing on the grass blade.

Roscoe attempted another cartwheel, ending in another flop. "I'm making a space machine," he informed me, flat on his back.

"Big deal," I said. "Do you realize you're lying on dog poop?"

Slow Roscoe rolled over, onto his skinny stomach, and inspected the grass. "Am not," he said, yanking out a handful of grass, then plucking a dandelion from the ground.

"Mama had a baby and its head popped off," Roscoe recited, snapping the yellow flower with his thumb.

"And that baby was *you*," I retorted. Roscoe ignored me.

"Did you know," he said, "that Wambchop will have a baby in about eight days?"

"Really?" I asked. "I thought she was just fat."

"Nope," said Roscoe. "Wambchop will be wambing soon."

"I love lambs," I said, smiling. "They're just about the cutest animals on earth."

Roscoe frowned. "They're not so cute being swaughtered, though," he said, wrinkling his big nose and sticking out his tongue. "Wambs are such big crybabies."

"Slaughtered?" I asked, catching my breath. "Don't tell me you kill *lambs?*"

Roscoe nodded. "Good eating," he said, picking at a scab on his knee. He flicked it into the dust, and the chickens came running.

I stood up, towering over Slow Roscoe, hands on hips and glaring. "You'll kill a lamb," I said, "over my dead body."

Roscoe cracked up. *Hiss, gasp, snuffle. Hiss, gasp, snuffle.*

"We wouldn't want your dead body, Wheezie," he said. "We couldn't eat *you.*"

I stomped off to the barn, Buford slobbering at my heels and Roscoe jabbering behind me.

"Stifle, Roscoe," I muttered, swinging open the barn door and striding into the straw. I made my way through the dark and hot stink to Lambchop's stall, where she lay fat and sweet, munching slow on something to eat.

"Baaaa," Lambchop bleated when she saw me, her big brown eyes soft and gentle.

"Hi, Lambchop," I said, climbing over the wooden slats and patting her head. I looked at her belly, big and full of baby.

"Don't worry, Lambchop," I whispered in her ear, wool tickling my lips. "There won't be a slaughter of the lambs, because I have a plan."

"Baaaa," said Lambchop again, searching my face with those eyes so warm and trusting.

"I have a plan," I said again, trying to convince myself along with Lambchop. "I'll save your baby's life, if it's the last thing I do on this stupid farm."

Chapter Eleven

One Small Step for Roscoe

Something was shining silvery bright through the trees, glaring in the sunlight as I headed to the dump with a boxful of junk.

"Backwoods hicks don't even have trash pickup," I groused, stomping through the sticks and watching for poison ivy. The dump was up ahead, at the end of the trail, and I fixed my eyes upon the silver shine, wondering what on earth could glitter so bright on top of that enormous heap of garbage.

The dump was a pile of Byler family trash from way back: tin cans and bedsprings and tiny little bottles that once held Listerine.

There were cough-drop tins and liniment tins and flea-powder tins, cracked Mason jars, and rusty toy cars, even an old porcelain doll, with a broken face and one arm, that once belonged to my mama.

"Littering in the woods like this should be against the law," I proclaimed. "Even if it *is* their own property." That's what Aunt Ida always said when I complained about the dump.

"It's our own property, Wheezie. Our land. And what else could we do with trash that can't be burned or fed to the animals or thrown in the garden for compost?" Aunt Ida got awful defensive about a dumb dump, if you asked me.

As I trudged closer to the dump, the silver shine hurt my eyes. I squinted, and shifted the box of trash in my arms, careful not to step on broken glass.

"Holy moley," I whispered, stopping dead in my tracks, "the old outhouse."

It was the rotten, falling-apart outhouse: the huge double-seater with carved half-moons and stars on the door. It used to belong to Granny and Gramps. Nobody could bear to throw the horrible thing away, even though my grandparents were gone.

The outhouse was covered top to bottom with tinfoil, crinkled up, taped on, and shining bright in the sunlight. "What kind of idiot would do something like this?" I whispered, dropping the box of junk and staring.

"The *Eagle* has wanded!"

"I should have known," I muttered, as Slow Roscoe stepped out from behind the silver outhouse, a roll of duct tape in his hand and a goofy grin on his stupid face.

"Hi, Wheezie," he said, "wike my space machine?"

Space machine. This was too much. Even Slow Roscoe couldn't be this dumb, to cover an outhouse with tinfoil in the middle of a dump, making believe it was a space machine.

"Come on in," said Roscoe, yanking open the door and giving a little bow like a butler at some fancy New York City hotel. "Be my guest. I cweaned it good with Ma's pine stuff."

Dumbfounded, I made my way across the tin cans and the bedsprings and the Listerine bottles, shaking my head. "Roscoe," I said, "how much tinfoil did you waste on this thing?"

Roscoe grinned, holding the door. "All those scraps that Ma's been saving," he said. "Awready-been-used tinfoil."

I wrinkled my nose, looking at the crinkly silver that wrapped the outhouse as if it were somebody's big stinky Christmas gift. "Roscoe," I said, "you're even weirder than I thought."

Roscoe guffawed. "A person has to be weird," he said, "to walk on the moon."

I rolled my eyes and stepped inside, the door slapping me in the behind as Roscoe let go. He came in behind me and perched over one of the holes on the seat. "The *Eagle* has wanded!" he hollered, bouncing up and down and jouncing around, making me think that maybe he'd fall right through the rotten floor and into the dump below.

"My astronaut seat," he said. "The assistant's seat," he added, pointing to the other toilet. I never could figure out why on earth people would want to sit side by side in an outhouse, making embarrassing noises and smells and doing things most folks prefer to do alone.

"That's your seat, Wheezie," said Roscoe, tapping the splintery wood. "You can be my assistant."

I snorted. "Roscoe," I said, "I need to be your assistant like this outhouse needs another seat."

"Hey," Roscoe said, his eyes big, "that would be neat. *Three* astronauts."

I rolled my eyes and went outside.

"Close the door, Wheezie," Roscoe said.

Sighing and griping to myself, I slammed the door and stepped back.

"Why?" I asked. "Time to fly to the moon?"

"No," said Roscoe. "Look up."

I tipped back my head and saw Roscoe's stupid blue eyes peering through two of the half-moon cutouts on top of the door. "My moon view," Roscoe said. "I'll be zooming through space, wooking through my moon view for that big white ball in the sky." He blinked his eyes, and I heard a thump as he jumped to the floor.

"The *Eagle* has wanded!" he shouted, then pushed open the door and bounced outside.

"One small step for Roscoe, one giant leap for mankind," he said, walking slowly across the dump with his arms bobbing out by his sides.

I snorted.

"The surface is fine and powdery and sticks to my boots wike charcoal," Roscoe said, lifting his bare foot and examining it.

"Your *brain* surface is fine and powdery," I said.

Roscoe grabbed a stick and planted it in the dump, among the junk, and then saluted. "Here Roscoe from the pwanet Earth first set foot upon the moon, August 1969. I come in peace for all mankind."

Roscoe scooped up Buford and made his way across the dump, heading for the out-house.

"This is Buford's hideout," he said, scoot-ing Buford inside. "A place where earth peo-ple would never find him."

And that's when I got the idea.

"Roscoe," I said, "remember when I said that I'd stop the slaughter of the lambs some-how?"

Roscoe nodded.

"Listen," I said, "I've got a plan."

Chapter Twelve

Partners in Crime

"Here's my plan," I said, talking plain and slow so Roscoe would understand.

"We take the lamb, when it's old enough to be away from Lambchop, and we hide it. We hide it somewhere nobody would ever find it." I paused, waiting for a light to flash on in Roscoe's murky mind. He just gawked at me, mouth open and a little bit of spit on his lips.

"We hide it somewhere that *earth people* never go," I said, waiting.

Roscoe thought, biting his lip, and then his eyes lit up. "Oh," he said, clapping his hands, "my space machine!"

72

"Right," I said, putting my arm around his shoulder. It was the first time I'd ever touched Slow Roscoe on purpose, but I figured I'd best butter him up if he was going to be my partner in crime.

"We take the lamb at night, when your parents are asleep," I continued, trying not to rest my arm too heavily on Roscoe's sweaty body.

Roscoe nodded.

"And then," I said, "we bring it here, to the space machine. We fix it up with some straw and some food and a nice warm blanket, and we raise it up to be a sheep. And then, when it's too old to be good to eat, you break the news to your pap and the sheep is released, to live on the farm forever and ever, like Lambchop."

Roscoe looked at me, buckteeth too close for comfort. "*I* break the news to Pap?" he asked.

I nodded, and carefully patted him on the back. "You get to do that," I said, "because I'll be gone."

"Gone?" asked Slow Roscoe.

"Gone," I said. "By the time the sheep is

too old to eat, I'll be back home, with Mama and Daddy." *Together*, I thought. *All of us together, maybe. I hope.*

Roscoe thought for a minute, gnawing on his lip. "But what if Ma and Pap hear the wamb crying for its mama?" he asked.

"They won't," I said, feeling like the smartest thing under the stars. "*We* always have to take out the trash, right?"

Roscoe nodded, looking back at the silver outhouse where Buford snored on the floor.

"Sounds wike a good pwan to me, Wheez-ie," he said. "You're so smart."

"And," I said, turning my head, "so are you." I took a deep breath of fresh air.

"Onwy *one* problem," said Roscoe, holding up a finger. "What do we do with the wamb when I wawk on the moon?"

I looked at Roscoe and smiled, which wasn't an easy feat with his face so close to mine.

"You take it with you," I said, practical as all get-out. "The first boy, dog, and lamb on the moon."

Roscoe tittered, and I slid my arm from his back, holding it out and away from the rest of my body.

"Not a baaaaa-d plan, huh?" I asked, and Roscoe cracked up.

"You are *so* funny, Wheezie," he said, slobbering and drooling.

I ignored him, heading fast for the house with my arm stiff at my side. I couldn't wait to scrub Slow Roscoe from my skin with some of Aunt Ida's lye soap.

Chapter Thirteen

Luna and the Moon

It was three boring weeks later, and the barn was as dark as the inside of a cow's belly. Roscoe kept stepping on my heels as we crept through the night in the direction of Lambchop and baby Luna's stall.

"Roscoe," I said, "turn on the flashlight."

"Not yet," Roscoe whispered. "I don't want to waste the batteries."

I stopped, and Roscoe smacked into my back.

"Ouch," he said, "my teeth."

"Well, if you'd keep them in your mouth where they're supposed to be . . ." I snapped.

"Why'd you stop, Wheezie?" whined Roscoe in my ear.

"Because I stepped in something squishy," I hissed, wiping my foot in the straw.

"Probably just cow poop," said Roscoe, and flicked on the light.

It was cow poop, all right. "Holy moley, Roscoe," I said, "do you think I want to *look* at cow manure between my toes? It's bad enough *feeling* the stuff, let alone *looking* at it. What are you trying to do, make me puke?"

"No," said Roscoe, pouting. He switched off the light and sniffled, his big nose next to my ear.

"I'm going outside," I said, "to wash my foot."

"No!" said Slow Roscoe. "You'll wake Ma."

"Well, then I'll go down to the duck pond in the back meadow," I said.

"NO!" said Roscoe, and turned on the light, beaming it up at his homely dough face. "Never, ever, ever in a million years go to the duck pond, Wheezie," he said, his face white and full of fear in the light. "Never, ever."

"Why not?" I asked, annoyed. Nothing makes me grouchier than manure between my toes.

"Because," said Roscoe, eyes scared and glaring, "the bulls will get you."

"The *bulls*," I mocked, making my eyes big and dopey. "Hogwash. Baloney. I'm not afraid of any stupid old bulls."

"I'm warning you, Wheezie," said Roscoe, turning off the flashlight. "Never, never, ever go to the duck pond."

"Well, where can I wash my foot?" I asked.

"In the water trough," said Roscoe.

"The *cows* drink out of that," I said, disgusted. "It's full of cow slobber."

Roscoe laughed. *Hiss, gasp, snuffle.* "Would you rather have swobber or poop?" he asked, and I made my way to the water trough, swishing my foot fast through the cool water.

"Let's go," I said, yanking my foot from the trough and dribbling water. "We have a lamb to steal."

Leading the way, I forged on to the stall, stumbling and fumbling through the night until I saw the outline of Lambchop's big fluffy head against the low window.

"Hi, Lambchop," I said, "remember my plan? I'm going to save your baby."

Lambchop bleated, a hoarse *baaa* in the dark.

"And don't worry," I said, climbing into the stall. "You will see Luna Lamb again, when she's too old to be good to eat. And then you'll be together forever."

"Forever and ever," chirped Roscoe, clicking on the flashlight and focusing the glow on Lambchop's baby.

Luna snuggled soft and fuzzy next to her mama, blinking in the light. I kneeled down and stroked her head, then circled her body with my arms.

"You'll see Mama again," I whispered, then heaved the lamb into my arms, pressing her warm against my chest. I took a deep breath and stood, grunting and swaying.

"Now how do I climb out of here?" I asked, Luna wiggling and bleating in my arms.

Hiss, gasp, snuffle. Hiss, gasp, snuffle. Slow Roscoe was in stitches for some stupid reason. "You'll have to hand her to me, Wheezie."

I buried my nose in Luna's wool, breathing in the new smell of unlived life. "Don't you dare drop her," I said, then hoisted the lamb over the wooden rail and into Roscoe's scrawny arms.

"The wamb has wanded!" Roscoe whispered as I vaulted over the slats and took Luna. Lambchop let loose with a loud *baaaaa*, then another and another, until the entire barn was filled with the sounds of her crying.

"Sssshhh," I whispered, making tracks toward the door, "you'll see her again, Lambchop."

Grunting and groaning, I lugged the lamb through the barn door and into the night, Roscoe blundering behind.

"Roscoe," I said, "you'd better not forget to take her back the minute she's too old to eat."

"There's something I forgot to tell you, Wheezie," said Roscoe. "We eat sheep, too."

"What?" I came to a halt, whipping around and glaring at Roscoe.

"Old sheep. It's called mutton. It's not as good as wamb, but it's okay."

Luna struggled in my arms. "Why didn't you ever eat Lambchop?" I asked, holding myself back from kicking Roscoe right in his knobby little knees.

"We use her milk," said Roscoe. "And sell her wool at shearing time. And she can have babies."

"So can Luna," I said, turning and making my way across the dewy grass. "Luna will have wool, and milk, and babies. Roscoe, I swear, you'd better take care of this lamb, once I'm gone."

"I will, Wheezie," said Roscoe, sliding his feet through the grass. "I promise."

"Cross your heart and hope to die?" I asked. "Swear on the *TV Guide*?"

"Yep," said Roscoe, and we walked on in silence. The moon was just a slice of white high in the sky, a fingernail clipping of fine and powdery stuff above us.

"Roscoe," I said, "if you had the chance, would you really walk on the moon?"

"Sure," said Roscoe, snapping a twig from a tree.

"Me, too," I said. Luna bleated, a soft and scared sound from somewhere deep inside her fuzzy body.

"We're almost there," I whispered, then shrieked. Something cold and wet brushed against my leg, then a tickle of fur. It was Buford, stupid Buford, bumbling along and trying to sniff Luna.

"Buford," I growled, "why must you always hound me, dogging my every footstep like some kind of *guard dog* or something?"

"Someday," Roscoe said, bending down and scooping Buford into his arms, "Wassie might save your life. Then you'll be sorry for all the mean things you say." He kissed Buford's head, smacking his big blubbery lips right between Buford's floppy ears.

We trekked on, Roscoe toting Buford and me holding Luna, up the trail and to the dump.

"Do you know," said Roscoe, "that the farther down you dig in this dump, the older stuff you find?"

"No kidding," I said. "Duh."

The silver outhouse—Roscoe's space machine—glimmered just ahead.

"Wheezie," said Roscoe, "we forgot something."

"What?" I snapped. My partner in crime was working on my nerves.

Roscoe took a breath. "The bwanket, food, and water," he said.

Chapter Fourteen

Nincompoops

"I hardly slept two winks all night, with Lambchop's racket," Aunt Ida ranted, having a conniption fit in the kitchen. "And somebody was rootin' through the attic in the middle of the night." Eyes wild and hair frizzed crazily around her face, Aunt Ida glared at Roscoe and me.

"That was me, Ma," said Roscoe. "I needed a bwanket."

"I think we should call the sheriff," Aunt Ida said, ignoring Roscoe. "Get those lamb bandits arrested."

"Calm down, Ida," said Uncle Ollie, slurping his coffee. "The lamb will be back, soon as the thieves get it through their heads that it's too new to be away from the mama."

"If the lamb doesn't die first," spat Aunt Ida, cracking eggs furiously into a bowl. "What kind of nincompoops would snitch a newborn lamb?"

Roscoe and I looked at each other across the table. "I think I'll head on outside," I said. "Such a beautiful morning."

"Me, too," slobbered Slow Roscoe, sliding back his chair.

Uncle Ollie smiled. "It's good to see you children becoming friends," he said.

I stuck out my tongue, pushing open the screen door and striding outside into the sunshine.

"Roscoe, you idiot," I said, as soon as we were out of earshot. "You moron. You said it was old enough to be away from the mama."

Roscoe pouted. "I don't know everything in the whole wide world," he said.

"That's an understatement," I remarked.

Looking back at the house, I made tracks across the yard and toward the dump, shaking my head the whole way. "Blockhead," I said. "Nitwit. Dumb little twit."

Roscoe hung his head and followed, looking for all the world like Buford being scolded by Aunt Ida.

I knew I was being mean, but I just couldn't seem to stop. "Kooky nincompoop," I said. "Luna is probably dead."

Roscoe stopped, a horrified look in his eyes. "If she is," he said, "it's your fault."

"*Your* fault, simpleton," I said. "You're the one who lives on a farm."

"So do you," said Roscoe. "All this summer."

"And I can't wait to get the heck out of here," I said. "Go home to *normal* folks."

"I can't wait for you to leave, either," said Roscoe. "You're so mean."

"And you're so stupid," I said, heading up the trail. "Believing that you're going to walk on the moon. Stupid, stupid, stupid." My heart was stinging beneath the Bee-Beautiful, as the image of a dead Luna buzzed again and again through my head. My mood ring was red, red and angry like the blood of all the innocent animals killed on this slaughterhouse of a farm.

"I don't know why I ever included you in

my plan," I went on. "I don't know why my parents ever shipped me off to your dumb farm, either. Grace, Pennsylvania, is the most boring place on earth, with nothing to do but watch TV and kill animals to pass the time. Boring, boring, boring."

Roscoe was silent, head hung as he shuffled along. If he had had a tail, it would have been dragging, that's how sad he looked. I decided to let up a bit.

"Sorry, Roscoe," I muttered, gritting my teeth and zeroing in on the silver outhouse. "I didn't mean to be so mean, but I will be as mad as a wet hen if Luna is dead."

"Not me," said Roscoe, quiet and pale. "I'll just be sad."

I stopped and looked at him, suddenly getting the picture that even Slow Roscoe had feelings inside of him. Somewhere beneath the buckteeth and greasy hair and bread-dough face, Roscoe had a heart and a soul and *feelings*, like everybody else.

"I really am sorry, Roscoe," I said. "I mean it."

Roscoe nodded, plucking at the skin on his elbow.

"Please be alive, Luna," I said, reaching for the outhouse door. *Please, please, please. I'll never be mean again, if I can help myself, and I'll try to smile and be nice to Roscoe, even if it kills me. I won't even call him Slow Roscoe anymore. Just please let Luna be okay.*

I pulled open the door, holding my breath, hands shaking. Luna was okay, she was fine, she was alive, looking up at me with soft brown eyes.

"The *Eagle* has wanded!" hollered Roscoe, and for once I bit my tongue, trying to be nice.

"Come on, Luna," I said, falling to my knees beside the lamb. "We're taking you back to your mama. But don't worry: I'll come up with another plan. A better plan."

Chapter Fifteen

Horse Sense

"Wheezie," snapped Aunt Ida, "I thought you had more horse sense."

Luna bleated and Roscoe disappeared, hiding somewhere behind the space machine.

"I . . . I'm sorry, Aunt Ida," I stammered, taking a step backward into the depths of the big outhouse. "I just wanted to save her from being slaughtered someday." I was beginning to wheeze, stuck in the outhouse beneath the gaze of Aunt Ida and the weight of Luna.

"Livin' on a farm, Wheezie, a soul gets used to slaughter," said Aunt Ida, shoving her hands deep into her pockets and scowling. "And anyway, it's not for you to decide which critters live and which die."

I hung my head, sinking down onto one of the seats and gently placing Luna on the floor.

"I had a hunch it was you," said Aunt Ida, "on account of the sheepish look in your eyes this mornin'."

"What about Roscoe?" I demanded. "He went along with the plan and helped to steal the lamb. He took a blanket from the attic, while I got some milk and water and stuff."

"Roscoe's slow," snapped Aunt Ida. "You're not."

"Roscoe lives on a farm," I said. "I don't." And it was then that I got the idea.

"Aunt Ida," I said, slow and careful, "I was wrong to take the lamb, and I'm sorry. I'm so sorry that I won't even blame you for sending me home right away." I took a long wheezing breath and crossed my fingers behind my back.

"Wheezie," said Aunt Ida, "I won't send you on home. But I am havin' you call your folks. You'll call your mama and daddy and

tell them just what you did last night." She
bent and lifted Luna, whipping around and
heading for the barn. "This critter could
have died," she said, throwing the words
over her shoulder as she walked away.

*So what, Aunt Ida? What do you care? You'll
kill Luna someday, anyway.* I dragged myself
from the outhouse and down the trail, glaring at Roscoe, who was still cowering behind
the space machine.

I poked along through the yard, until I
saw Aunt Ida bustling from the barn and
heading for the house. "To the telephone,
Wheezie," she hollered, and I saw Uncle Ollie shaking his head in the doorway.

"Did you do what she thought you might
have done?" he asked, quiet and gentle, and
I nodded.

Uncle Ollie smiled, then patted me on the
shoulder as I headed for the telephone.

"Daddy?" I said when he answered.

"Hi, honey!" Daddy said, his voice happy
and glad. "How are you doing?"

"Not so good," I whispered, Aunt Ida's
eyes boring holes in my back. "I stole a
lamb."

"You *what?*" Daddy asked, almost laughing.

"I took a new lamb from its mama and hid it in the outhouse," I said, my words tumbling out and falling over one another. "I wanted to save it from being killed someday, so Roscoe and I stole it and hid it. And Aunt Ida found out."

"Well," said Daddy, a smile in his voice, "I'll bail you out of jail."

I took a deep breath, feeling the wheeze deep in my chest. "Is Mama there?" I asked.

Daddy paused. "No," he said, "she's not."

My heart clenched. "Are you two *ever* there at the same time?" I asked.

"No, honey," said Daddy, "not very often."

I turned, seeing that Aunt Ida had left the room. I was alone, all by myself with Daddy and the telephone.

"Daddy," I said, "I think I should come home. Soon. I have asthma, and I've become a woman, and now I'm in trouble with Aunt Ida, and I can't stand Roscoe. All he ever does is watch TV and holler, Daddy. And Uncle Ollie is always busy killing animals, and all they eat is meat. Meat, meat, meat. I hate it."

There was a click, and I knew Evie Nettle had her ear glued to the telephone.

"You used to like meat," Daddy said, all common sense and calm.

And you used to like Mama, I thought. "I don't like it now," I said.

"Oh, well," said Daddy, "people change. You don't have to eat meat if you don't like it. Just make sure you get enough protein and iron from other foods, okay, honey?"

"Okay," I sighed.

"And," said Daddy, "don't go stealing any more lambs." He laughed, and there was a sharp breath from Evie Nettle.

"Don't worry," I said. "I have more horse sense than that." We said our good-byes and hung up, and then I went upstairs to find my inhaler, all full of horse sense and wheezes and missing Mama and Daddy.

Chapter Sixteen

A Night Dark as Deep Water

It was a night dark as deep water, with hardly a moon in the sky, and we were watching a new show called "Hee Haw."

"Hee, hee, hee," Roscoe sang. "Hee, hee, hee. Hee, hee, hee, haw, haw, haw, haw."

"What talent, Roscoe," I remarked.

"That dog on TV puts me in mind of Buford," said Roscoe.

"Fat and lazy," I commented, stretching out across the floor. I despised "Hee Haw," with its country-hick jokes and singing hillbillies, but there was nothing better to do. I yawned, and my stomach growled. I'd only had some corn and rhubarb sauce for supper, as ham was the main course.

Minnie Pearl pranced across the stage, wearing a hat dangling with price tags. Roscoe cracked up, actually rolling on the floor and holding his sides. "That wady is *so* funny," he said.

"You know, Roscoe, there won't be TV on the moon," I said.

Roscoe stopped rolling. "Hey," he said, "I never thought of that. I won't stay wong, if there's no tewevision."

"Oh, take your time, Roscoe," I said. "It's not every day you get to walk on the moon."

Roscoe fixed his eyes on the screen, gawking at a goofy couple trying to hang a picture on a wall. The picture kept falling off, and Roscoe guffawed, slapping his scrawny knees.

"Hey, Ma," he said, when a commercial blared into the room, "we need to get a new frame for that picture of Granny and Gramps. It fell off the wall in Wheezie's room."

Aunt Ida nodded, crocheting away in her rocking chair. She'd been working on that blanket forever, it seemed.

Uncle Ollie cleared his throat. "Don't take this to heart," he said, "but there's an old wives' tale, a superstition, that if a picture falls from the wall for no reason, that means somebody is goin' to die."

"Somebody dies all the time," Roscoe said with a shrug.

"Somebody *close*, Roscoe," I said, trying hard to keep a nice tone of voice.

Roscoe looked around the room. "You're all close," he said.

"It's only a superstition," Uncle Ollie said. "Don't take it to heart."

"Hee Haw" flashed back on, and a lady popped her head from a cornfield, acting all perky and country-fresh. If only people knew what living in the sticks was *really* like, they wouldn't be so all-fired excited about this stupid new show. I'd rather watch reruns of Lawrence Welk leading his boring orchestra than waste time on this hogwash. Nonetheless, I stayed planted on the floor: a bump on a log in Grace, Pennsylvania.

"I Love 'Hee Haw,' " Roscoe announced, clapping his hands and bobbing his head.

Uncle Ollie belched.

"Bless you," said Aunt Ida, crocheting

away, as Roscoe clapped and Buford gnawed on his stub of a tail.

I must have the strangest relatives of anybody in the whole wide world, I thought, seeing them with the eyes of somebody else for a minute. I hated to admit it, but I was almost getting accustomed to their strange ways.

"I'm gwad the Vietnam War Show isn't on tonight," Roscoe said. "I hate that show."

"Roscoe," I said from between clenched teeth, "the Vietnam War isn't a show."

The words were barely out of my mouth before the Jesus picture dropped. Just fell fast from the wall behind Aunt Ida and crashed to the floor, Jesus still knocking at a door.

We all stared at the picture, faceup on the floor, and then at one another.

"That hung there for years," Uncle Ollie said, rubbing his bald head.

"Since before Roscoe was born," added Aunt Ida, craning her neck to look back at the painting that had once belonged to Granny.

"Wucky it didn't have gwass," said Roscoe. "Wonder who's going to die?"

"That's just a superstition," said Uncle Ollie, and then he heaved himself off the sofa and limped to the picture, picking it up and hanging it back in place.

"Straight?" he asked, tilting Jesus left, then right.

I nodded, feeling goose bumps prickle across my arms and sweat drip from my head. The train whistled in the distance, the sound sifting through the screen window and lingering in the room.

"Must be a storm comin'," Aunt Ida remarked.

"I hope the ewectric doesn't go off until 'Hee Haw' is over," Roscoe said.

A roll of thunder rumbled across the sky, and Buford started barking to beat the band. Running in circles and yipping with a crazy look in his eyes, he put me in mind of what a dog with rabies must be like.

"Buford!" yelled Aunt Ida. "Lie down."

Buford didn't lie down; he skittered to the window and stared out into the night, eyes bright and tail still. Then he began to howl like a wolf or a coyote, nose held high and wailing. A light swept the room, and Buford bolted for the kitchen door, barking like some kind of a guard dog or something.

"What on earth has got into that dog?" asked Aunt Ida, standing and draping the blanket across the rocking chair. "Somebody must have pulled into the drive," she said, peering through the window.

"I heard a car door," Uncle Ollie remarked from his place on the sofa.

Roscoe just gawked at "Hee Haw," eyes wide and mouth open.

Aunt Ida sighed. "Who would be here this time of night?" she asked. "Wheezie, come and hold Buford, would you?"

I nodded and followed her to the kitchen, where Buford was attacking the screen door. Aunt Ida flipped on the porch light, and there was rain and two men blinking in the light.

"Ida Byler?" asked one of the men, tall and straight in some kind of blue suit uniform.

Aunt Ida nodded, pushing open the door and stepping out onto the porch. I watched, nose pressed against the screen and Buford barking in my arms.

"And Oliver?" asked the other man, short and straight in the same type of suit. The suits were not like any I'd ever seen on TV, and neither were the looks on the men's faces. A shiver ran through me as Aunt Ida turned to the door.

"Ollie," she hollered, "two fellas here to see you."

Uncle Ollie lumbered into the kitchen, a searching look wrinkling his face. He limped to the door, brows drawn tight and eyes narrow.

"Oliver Byler?" asked Tall and Straight. "Brother of Obadiah?"

Uncle Ollie nodded, slow, and I could hear his breath, shaky and scared.

"Officers of the United States military, sir," said Short and Straight, saluting and pulling a piece of paper from his pocket. "We have been sent by the government, along with deepest regrets, to inform you that Private Obadiah Byler, missing in action since June 8, 1968, has lost his life in service to his country. We're very sorry, sir, . . . ma'am, . . . miss."

With those words, everything stopped,

leaving nothing but the rain, the men, the light, and a night dark as deep water. I gasped for air, feeling as if I were drowning, and Buford whimpered in my arms.

And that's when Aunt Ida fainted, hitting the porch at the shiny black shoes of the men in suits.

Chapter Seventeen

The Ten Hardest Words

Uncle Ollie bent over Aunt Ida, and I paced circles in the kitchen, taking deep breaths. *Uncle Ob is dead, gone, never to be seen again.* It seemed like a dream, a bad dream that goes on and on. I walked and walked, drawing in breaths, and thinking how Uncle Ob would never take a breath or a step again, not on this earth, anyway.

Aunt Ida was sitting up and the men in suits were gone, leaving behind the terrible news they'd brought. Free and relieved, they'd taken off and left us alone to deal with the grief.

Buford was still in my arms and I held

him close, needing to be near to his breath and the steady thump of his heart. The cuckoo clock hooted and "Hee Haw" blared in the living room, making me wonder how life goes on with death so close. Roscoe clapped and laughed, and Buford flopped to the floor, pitter-pattering sad and slow across the linoleum, as if he knew.

Roscoe. Roscoe doesn't know. I closed my eyes for a moment, then staggered to the living room door.

"Roscoe," I said, my voice tight. Roscoe looked at me, a question bulging in his eyes.

"Uncle Ob died, Roscoe. He died in the Vietnam War." Those ten words were the hardest words I ever said in my life, and left me feeling empty, as if somebody had poked a hole in my soul and drained it.

Roscoe drew a sharp breath, grabbing his chest. "*Ob* died?" he asked, and I nodded.

Roscoe burst into sobs, loud and aching. "He always pwayed checkers with me," he blurted, snot gushing from his nose and his face blotching red and splotchy. "And rummy and Monopowy and go fish and war. He never poked fun at me, and he gave me hugs. *Ob* can't be dead." Roscoe buried his face between his knees and cried his eyes out, wailing and keening and weeping, beating his hands fast and hard upon the floor.

"I hate the Vietnam War," he blubbered, and something inside me broke. I let loose the sadness in my throat, and it exploded out my eyes, then my mouth, then my heart.

"I hate it, too," I howled. "I hate it, I hate it, I hate it." I collapsed on the floor beside Roscoe, and we bawled like babies, screaming at the top of our lungs.

And then I hugged him. Just reached out and pulled him close, not caring about his sweat or his bad breath or the snot dripping from his nose. I held him close, our tears mingling and our hearts breaking, until he stopped shaking. "Hee Haw" was coming to an end, and I stood and turned off the television, staring at the little white dot on the screen until it disappeared.

"I can't believe he's really gone," I said. "It seems like maybe he's still in Vietnam, just lost or something."

Roscoe looked at me, wiping his eyes and snuffling. "I wish he was," he said.

I didn't say anything, just twisted the copper band on my wrist. *OB, Obadiah Byler, MIA 6/8/68.* He was still missing, just not in action anymore, and everything was changed. Funny how a few words can come from out of the blue and make things black.

"I'm going to call your mother, Wheezie." It was Uncle Ollie, slumped in the doorway and looking ten years older than he looked ten minutes ago.

I nodded. "Tell her I love her," I said. "Is Aunt Ida okay?"

Uncle Ollie nodded. "She went upstairs to bed," he said. "We all need a good night's sleep, because," he paused and took a deep breath, "the officers said that Ob's body is being flown in to the airport in Philadelphia tomorrow."

And that's when Roscoe leaped up and bolted outside, bursting into the rainy night as if he could make it disappear.

Chapter Eighteen

Broken Hopes

I found him in his space machine, huddled on the floor and weeping.

"Roscoe," I said, rain pelting my face as I stood in the doorway, Uncle Ollie's flashlight grasped in my hand.

Roscoe ignored me, and his cries seemed to shake the space machine as thunder shook the sky. I looked up, and began shivering and trembling like the wet leaves on the trees above us. *Uncle Ob is gone.* I could still see his smile and hear his voice, and now he was gone.

"Roscoe," I said again, stepping into the outhouse, "are you going to be okay?" I reached over and touched his shoulder.

"I'll never be okay," Roscoe said, sobbing. "Not without Ob."

I sank down to the floor beside him as a rush of rain pummeled the space machine and lightning flashed and crackled. We sat like that for a long time, quiet and crying and hunched side by side, until Roscoe broke the silence.

"Why would they fwy his *body* in on an airplane?" he asked. "What do we want with his body, if Ob isn't in it?"

I sighed. "So we can say good-bye. So we can see it and know that Ob is really and truly dead. So we can accept." I rubbed my eyes, feeling full of broken hopes and wishing I was dreaming.

Roscoe looked at me through the damp and muggy dark. "Do you think there'll be a funeral?" he asked.

"I'm sure," I said.

"Well, I won't be going," declared Roscoe. "I want to remember Uncle Ob the way he *really* was, not how he wooks in some box."

There was a whimper outside and I jumped, startled. Roscoe stretched out his foot and kicked open the door. It was Buford, smelling like wet dog and climbing inside.

"Hi, Buford," whispered Roscoe. "Uncle Ob is dead. He died in the Vietnam War." Buford whimpered again and settled on Roscoe's lap, his nose cold on my shoulder.

"Why do we have war, Wheezie?" Roscoe asked.

I thought for a while. "I guess for the same reasons we have divorce: because sometimes people just can't get along. They fight and they fight and they fight, each thinking they're right and the other one wrong."

"And maybe they're *both* wrong," Roscoe said.

"Or maybe they're both *right*," I said with a shrug. "But in the end it just doesn't matter anymore, because everybody gets hurt anyway."

"Divorce is stupid," said Roscoe, "but war is stupider."

I sighed and stood, grief heavy in my legs and tiredness fogging up my head. "I'm going for a walk, Roscoe," I said.

Roscoe nodded, trailing me through the door and into the drizzly dark. He stopped dead in his tracks, gazing straight ahead with rain splashing his face, and then he whipped out his hand and ripped a piece of tinfoil from the outhouse. Breathing hard, Roscoe crumpled the foil and hurled it to the ground, screaming without sound.

"Roscoe," I gasped, "stop."

Tearing fast and furious, Roscoe yanked piece after piece of the shiny wrapping from his space machine and crushed it to nothingness in his hands, his hair hanging heavy and wet across his eyes and tiny balls of foil piled at his feet.

"I don't need a space machine," Roscoe said. "I'm never going to walk on the moon. Never . . . ever . . . ever."

That's when I took flight and lit off into the night, fleeing Roscoe and his broken hopes.

Chapter Nineteen

Roscoe Is Always Right

I ran like the wind, beneath the black sky and across slick grass, rain racing down my face and a picture sticking in my mind. It was Ob, Easter Eve of 1963, slumped on the rocking chair beneath the Jesus picture, bawling his eyes out because Granny was gone. I was six; Ob was thirteen and as big as the sky to me.

"Why can't you stop crying, Uncle Ob?" I asked, sitting on the floor at his feet.

Ob just shook his head, not answering, and I was too dumb to understand how it must have felt to lose two parents in one year.

And now I was the one who couldn't stop crying.

Breathing deep, I slid beneath the back meadow fence, squishing through the mud toward the duck pond. Roscoe's warning echoed in my memory: *Never, ever, ever in a million years go to the duck pond, Wheezie. Never, ever, ever.*

It seemed like a million years since Roscoe had said those words and taken Luna to the space machine. What silly kids we'd been, just a few days ago. Things that had been so important then didn't even matter now, in the shadow of Ob's death. I shook off Roscoe's warning, thinking that maybe doing something foolhardy would take the edge off my grief.

I was up to my shins in mud, sloshing through the back meadow and seeing the dark oval of the duck pond ahead. Ducks were swimming, skimming silent and smooth, blurs of white moving peacefully through the night. I sat on the bank and watched, rain seeping into my clothes and making circles in the pond below. I was muddy, wet, tired, and sad, sadder than I'd ever been in my life.

The rain slowed and some stars poked their way through the black, sparkling silver and bright in the night. A duck quacked, and I stood, stripping down to my underwear and making my way to the water.

Wading in, I watched the ducks cluster, and then I dove, splashing through the soothing cool water. I swam and swam, stroking laps back and forth across the pond as the ducks gawked and the rain stopped.

Coming to a halt, I saw a shadow on the other side of the water. A *big* shadow, with fur and a tail and horns that jutted tall and sharp into the sky. *A bull*. Heart hammering, I climbed from the pond and hightailed it up the slippery bank, heading for my clothes.

And then it happened—in a rush of fur and hooves and stomping and snorting—the bull lowered his horns and charged, barreling toward me with the speed of greased lightning. I shrieked and headed for a tree, grabbing fast to a branch and hoisting myself into the V. "Help!" I screamed, clinging to a limb and hanging on for dear life as the bull rammed the trunk of the tree beneath me.

"Help! Somebody help me!" I began to sob, trying to climb higher as the bull got madder and the night got blacker.

"Please . . . PLEASE . . . HELP!" I wailed at the top of my lungs, my life flashing before my eyes as I'd always heard happens just before death. "HELP . . . HELP . . ." It felt like forever came and went, in those moments of yelling my head off and begging for help.

"We're coming, Wheezie!" It was Roscoe, stumbling through the meadow with Buford barking at his heels. Buford saw the bull and went berserk: running like a shot, barking and snapping and growling and attacking. Finally, the bull turned tail and disappeared, thundering off into the night.

I started to shake and couldn't stop, fear and relief choking my throat and jolting through my body. I tried to talk, but no words came out, so I just clung to the tree like a locust shell, mouth open and eyes closed.

"Wheezie Moore, come on down!" hollered Roscoe.

"I . . . I . . . can't," I stammered. "I can't move."

"Hurry," said Roscoe, "before more bulls come."

I gathered my wits and then jumped, dropping to the ground in a thud of mud and wet grass. Head pounding and heart jarred, I curled up into a ball of dullness, like one of Roscoe's scrunched-up pieces of tinfoil. "You two saved my life," I whispered, as Buford nuzzled my head. "Thank you."

"I *told* you never, ever, ever go to the duck pond," Roscoe said, wagging a finger at me. "And I told you Buford might save your life someday. Roscoe is always right." He raised his hand to his lips, fingers curled under, and blew on his nails, buffing them on his shoulder. "I told you so," he said, smugness and arrogance dripping from his lips.

I didn't answer, just folded my knees to my nose and shivered, still seeing that blur of fur and horns racing full tilt through the night.

"Say it five times," Roscoe commanded. "Roscoe is always right."

"Roscoe is always right," I gasped, fast

and quiet. "Roscoe is always right, Roscoe is always right, Roscoe is always right."

"That was only four times," Roscoe said.

"Roscoe is always right," I said, taking a deep breath and pulling myself up. Roscoe grabbed the flashlight and flicked it on, blinding me with the beam.

"Yuck!" said Roscoe, covering his eyes. "Why are you onwy wearing underwear?"

"It's a long story," I responded, snatching up my muddy clothes and squirming into them.

"Wheezie wears a bee bra, Wheezie wears a bee bra," Roscoe taunted, as we made tracks through the muddy meadow and into the yard, my guard dog, Buford, leading the way.

I ignored Roscoe, looking at the darkened house and thinking of how Aunt Ida and Uncle Ollie had no idea that they'd just about lost a niece.

"Imagine," I said, shaking my head, "I could have been *dead*." I shuddered at the feel of the word in my mouth, so hard and cold and sad.

Stopping in the muck, I was struck by a

thought. "If I'd been killed by that bull," I mused, "you could bet your sweet bippy that Mama and Daddy wouldn't even *think* about a divorce. They'd be sorry then, all right. Why, I bet they'd stay together forever, mired in grief and regret and sorrow, if anything ever happened to me."

Roscoe just shrugged, squishing mud through his toes and then rubbing them across Buford's back.

"Roscoe," I said, hooking my arm in his, "I have a plan."

"Not again," Roscoe whined. "I hate your pwans."

"Roscoe," I said, putting my arm around him, "this plan is important. It might just keep my parents from getting a divorce."

Roscoe pulled away and the night was quiet, except for Buford, snuffling in the wet grass.

"The wast time I helped with one of your pwans," Roscoe pouted, "you called me all kinds of names: kooky nincompoop and stupid and moron and idiot and nitwit and dumb wittle twit and bwockhead and simpleton and . . ."

"Roscoe," I said, "I'm sorry. I'm sorry

for everything mean I ever said, and everything mean I ever did. I honestly am
sorry."

Roscoe was beginning to sniffle, and he
plopped down on the porch steps, burying
his head between his knees.

"I miss Ob," he blurted, starting to sob.

I took a deep breath, my insides quivering
and my outsides shivering. "Me, too," I said,
sinking down onto the step beside Roscoe.
Buford crawled into my arms, his stub still
and nose cold.

Roscoe snorted, swiping at his eyes. "I
didn't really miss him until tonight," he said.
"I just pretended that everything would be
aw right. Vietnam is so far away, you
know."

I didn't say anything, just pressed my
mouth to the copper band on my wrist.

Roscoe clenched his fists. "I'm not going
awong to get Ob's body tomorrow," he said.
"No way. Not even if Ma and Pap paddle
me a trillion times, or ground me until I'm a
grown-up. I'm not going: never, ever, ever
in a million years." A slow rumble of thunder rolled across the sky, and the train whistle sounded, urgent and loud.

"I'm . . . not . . . going," Roscoe chanted, pounding his fists on his bony knees.

"Me neither," I said, then paused, trembling. "Here's my plan, Roscoe," I said, soft and slow. "Tonight, we run away."

Chapter Twenty

Running Away

By the beam of Uncle Ollie's best flashlight, we packed Roscoe's old red wagon. It was piled high: two sleeping bags, two pillows, clothes, toilet paper, shampoo, a loaf of bread and a jug of red punch, a butter tub filled with dog food for Buford, two cakes of Aunt Ida's lye soap, a stack of *TV Guides*.

"Roscoe," I said, "why on earth do you need a bunch of moldy old *TV Guides*?"

Roscoe shrugged as I flicked off the flashlight and tucked it between the sleeping bags.

"I need something to read," he said as I lifted the handle and yanked on the wagon.

It creaked and rattled as we walked across the yard, away from the house.

"Sshhh," I hissed, pulling slow and careful. That was all we needed: to have our plan ruined by a stupid wagon now that we'd gotten this far. Roscoe and I had sneaked into the house, as silent as the stars. We'd washed up, then gathered all the stuff we needed to live on our own for a while. Everything necessary for running away. *Running away.* The words chugged circles around my brain like a toy train—again and again—sending chills down my spine and a sharp feeling into my heart. I never in all my days would have believed that I—Louise Olivia Moore— would be *running away* from the very people who gave me my name. And my life. Served them right, though, for ever *thinking* about divorce.

"Good-bye, house," Roscoe said, turning around and waving. "Good-bye, Ma and Pap." He sniffled. "Good-bye, farm. Good- bye, chickens and sheep and bulls and crickets and ducks."

"For heaven's sake, Roscoe," I said, disgusted, "we're not leaving *forever*. Just long enough to scare the daylights and the divorce out of my parents."

Roscoe sighed. "I hate good-byes," he said, then slapped his head.

"We forgot something, Wheezie," he said. "Something important."

"What?" I asked. "Your brain?"

Roscoe ignored me, stumbling toward the outkitchen with Buford at his heels. He disappeared inside for a few minutes as I stood tapping my foot beside the wagon. When he came back out, something glinted silver in the night.

"The Chicken Killing Ax," Roscoe announced, planting it between the pillows.

"What do we need that for?" I asked, rolling my eyes and reaching for the wagon handle.

"Maybe to swaughter some food," Roscoe said. "Or to fight off bad guys or coyotes or big snakes. We might need it to wive off the wand."

I shook my head, dragging the wagon past the barn, past the shed, and into the woods.

"Hey, Wheezie," Roscoe said, "where are we running away to, anyway?"

"Well," I said, feeling like a big shot, "I thought we'd sleep tonight in your space machine, then spend tomorrow looking for somewhere farther away. Somewhere they'd never find us."

Roscoe scratched his armpit. "What if Ma brings some trash to the dump in the morning?" he asked.

"She won't," I said. "They'll be in a hurry to get to the airport. Anyway, that's *our* chore . . . remember?"

Roscoe yawned. "I'm tired," he said. "I never stayed up this wate before."

I yawned, too, as we lugged the wagon on the trail and across the dump, crunching over tin cans and bedsprings and jars. "The *Eagle* has wanded!" Roscoe hollered, as we approached the outhouse, hulking dark and circled with balls of tinfoil.

"Ssshhh," I hissed. "You'll wake the dead."

Roscoe looked at me. "Stop it, Wheezie," he whined. "You're scaring me."

I rolled my eyes, yanking open the outhouse door and pushing the wagon inside.

"Give me a hand, Roscoe," I said. "We need to lift the wagon up onto the seat."

"Why do we need the wagon inside?" asked Roscoe, watching Buford pee in the weeds.

"In case it rains again, stupid," I snapped, too tired to put up with Roscoe's dumb questions. "Plus we don't want anybody who might happen by to see it."

Roscoe pouted. "See, I told you that every time I help you with a pwan, all you do is call me names." He kicked at a stick on the floor.

"Sorry," I muttered, picking up one end of the wagon while Roscoe heaved on the other end. We lifted it up onto the seat, placing the wheels on either side of the holes.

And then, on a night as dark as deep water, Roscoe and I arranged our sleeping bags and pillows on the floor of the outhouse and fell fast asleep, dreaming of running away.

Chapter Twenty-one

Missing Persons

I woke to the chirping of birds, sunlight slanting through the cracks of the outhouse, and Roscoe's breath blowing in my face. Buford was sleeping on my stomach.

Roscoe rolled over, mumbling, and then passed gas. I stared at the back of his greasy head, as Buford licked Roscoe's bread-dough face.

"This is the most disgusting morning in history," I grumbled, gazing up at the cobwebs on the ceiling and the loaded wagon balanced across the seat.

"Good morning, Wheezie," Roscoe sputtered, flipping over and flashing me one of his goofy bucktoothed grins. "I swept pretty good."

"Well, I hope you didn't pee your pants," I remarked. "Sleeping bags don't come with plastic sheets."

"Shut up," said Roscoe. "Stifle."

I stood, rubbing my eyes and rolling up my sleeping bag. "I bet it's about nine o'clock already," I said, tossing my sleeping bag and pillow into the wagon. I stepped outside, taking a deep breath of fresh air. Buford followed, whizzing in the weeds, then looked at me and wagged his stub of a tail.

"Good morning, Buford," I said. "Thanks again for saving my life last night."

"And me," fussed Roscoe, stumbling through the door. "I helped too, Wheezie." He bumbled into the woods, hid behind a tree, and peed.

"Gross," I said, as Roscoe stepped out and up onto the dump, tugging on his zipper.

"One small step for man," he said, teetering across the trash. "One *gigantic* leap for Wheezie and Buford and me. We run away in peace for all mankind: August 1969."

"You're weird, Roscoe," I said. My stomach growled.

"Let's go down to the house and get something to eat," I said, running my fingers through the knots in my hair.

Roscoe gawked at me. "We can't go back home, Wheezie," he said. "We're running *away*."

"We're not gone yet," I said. "I need a good breakfast."

"But Ma and Pap will make us *stay*," Roscoe said, wrinkling his forehead.

"Dummy," I said, "they're already gone."

"See, Wheezie," whined Roscoe, "you're cawing me names again. I'm going home. I'm not running away with you. Come on, Wassie." He smacked his drooling lips, patted his scrawny leg, and lit off through the woods, Buford waddling along behind.

"Wait!" I called. "I'm sorry, Roscoe. I'll never do it again: cross my heart and hope to die." I crossed my fingers behind my back and followed, thinking of the conniption fits Uncle Ollie and Aunt Ida would throw if Roscoe reached home before they'd left and ran his mouth about my plan.

"Roscoe," I said, catching up and putting

my arm around his shoulders, "I'm sorry." I held my breath as Roscoe bit his lip and scrunched up his nose and squinted his eyes.

"That's okay," he finally said. "Just don't do it again."

We headed down the trail, past the barn and the shed, and toward the house. Uncle Ollie's big green car was gone and the farm was quiet, only Luna making noise in the barn. "Nobody's home, Roscoe," I said, bounding up the steps and into the kitchen.

"I bet they were worried sick, once they noticed we were missing," I remarked, flopping onto a red vinyl chair and flipping through a stack of mail. Nothing good: only a newspaper and a new *TV Guide*. "I bet they already called my parents and the police," I added, feeling my heart skip a beat. "Why, search parties are probably raking the state for us, Roscoe, from here to my house. We'll be on the news and everything."

"On TV?" Roscoe asked, his eyes all lit up.

"Yep," I said, nodding. "And on missing persons' posters down at the post office. Old Evie Nettle will be poking her nose into those, all right." I snickered as the cuckoo clock hooted nine times and Roscoe moseyed into the living room, switching on the television.

"Wheezie," he called, " 'Mister Ed' is on. Not us."

I ignored him, reaching for a sheet of paper propped against the salt and pepper shakers. It was a note, in Aunt Ida's sloppy handwriting.

Wheezie and Roscoe: We went to Philadelphia to meet the plane and follow the hearse on home. You children were up and playing already by the time we left, so I thawed some scrapple in the icebox for your breakfast. It's good cold. Don't forget to feed chickens and slop hogs. Be home by suppertime.

I sighed, shaking my head. They didn't even know we were gone. Well, they'd know tonight, along with the rest of Pennsylvania. I picked up the phone and dialed the Grace County Sheriff's Department, staring at the numbers Aunt Ida posted on the wall beside the phone.

"Hello," I said when the man answered, "I'd like to report some missing persons."

Chapter Twenty-two

Somewhere Close, but Far Enough

"Who did you say was calling?" asked Roscoe, gnawing on a hunk of scrapple.

"Ida Byler," I said, making my voice all hoarse and low like Aunt Ida's.

Roscoe guffawed. "You sound just like Ma," he said, chewing with his mouth open.

I poured a bowl of Cheerios, thinking how I'd need all the energy I could get for running away.

"I told him that the missing persons were most likely headed for Wheezie's home," I said, slicing a banana and chugging milk into the bowl. "Told him all about how the poor girl's folks are thinking about getting a divorce, against her best wishes, and how she probably was running away from Grace and home to Mama."

"So what are they going to do?" Roscoe asked, pieces of brown mush smattered across his chin.

"Look for us," I said with a grin, thinking of Mama and Daddy leading the search party, *together*. And then they'd *stay* together, once they knew what it would feel like to lose me. Together forever, the way it should be.

"So what are *we* going to do?" Roscoe asked.

I thought for a minute, crunching Cheerios. "Run away," I said, shrugging. "Somewhere close, but far enough for them to get good and worried."

"And we'll stay away until the funeral is over," Roscoe declared, flicking a piece of scrapple to Buford. "There's no way I'm going to look at Ob in some box. Never, ever, ever in a million years."

I picked up the newspaper, wondering if Ob's picture was on the obituary page. I hated that page, the way they shrunk people's lives down to a fuzzy photograph topping off a couple of paragraphs of words. A whole life, condensed to about four inches of black and white.

"Hey, Wheezie," Roscoe said, pointing, "look what's on the front page."

GRACE COUNTY FAIR TODAY, said the headline. I loved the Grace County Fair: the merry-go-round and the Ferris wheel and the moon walk and the bumper cars and the cotton candy and the caramel apples. One day and night of magic, all crammed into a midway set up at the intersection of Cowpoke and Slowpoke roads, about two miles the way the crow flies from the farm.

I held the newspaper to my heart as Roscoe stuck the *TV Guide* under his arm and moseyed to the sink with his dirty plate.

"Let's get a move on, Roscoe," I said. "We've got to get out of here fast, before somebody comes from the sheriff's department."

"Where are we going, Wheezie?" asked Roscoe.

"Just hurry up, Roscoe," I ordered. "I have a plan."

I knew exactly where we were headed: somewhere close, but far enough.

Chapter Twenty-three

Wheezie Is Always Right

Chugging down Cowpoke Road on Uncle Ollie's tractor, I glanced back at the wagon, tied to the tractor hitch with a rope Roscoe had found in the barn. As I held tight to the steering wheel, I craned my neck to see around Roscoe, perched on the front of the tractor with Buford in his arms.

"The *Eagle* has wanded!" Roscoe hollered. "We're running away!"

"Stifle, Roscoe!" I yelled over the sputtering of the tractor. Evie Nettle's red, white, and blue Jeep was putting down the road, Evie's busybody face gawking at us through the windshield.

I waved, faking a smile. "Just taking the tractor over to the Cow Corn!" I shouted, slowing down and pointing to the plot Uncle Ollie called the Cow Corn. "Plowing a few more rows for Uncle Ollie." Evie nodded, slow and nosy, and turned to watch as I guided the tractor into the little field across the road, where Uncle Ollie grew corn for the cows.

"Bye, Evie Nettle!" I hollered in my best fake voice. "Nosy old busybody," I commented, as she putted away.

Roscoe turned to look at me, buckteeth gleaming in the sunlight and greasy hair blowing in the breeze. Buford turned, too, ears flapping and tail wagging.

"We're running away!" Roscoe hollered again, and then he started to sing the theme song from "The Beverly Hillbillies," changing the words to something about packing the wagon and stealing the tractor and heading to California.

"Stifle, Roscoe," I muttered, making a U-turn between the cornstalks and bumping through the dirt and onto the road.

We chugged along for what seemed like

forever; then finally I smelled the french fries. We were there: the Grace County Annual Fair.

I parked the tractor in the woods behind the fair, and Roscoe and Buford leaped from the front and onto the ground.

"You drove good, Wheezie," said Roscoe. "Did you ever drive a tractor before?"

"Nope," I answered, hopping down and checking the wagon. "There's a first time for everything."

"Why did we drive?" asked Roscoe. "Why didn't we just walk?"

"Too hot for walking," I said. "We can't afford to waste all that energy."

"Well, I don't know if it was a very good idea, Wheezie," Roscoe said. "Pap will be awful mad."

I waved away his words. "Wheezie is always right," I said. "Say it five times."

"Wheezie is always right, Wheezie is always right, Wheezie is always right," Roscoe chanted as we walked across the field, Buford dashing ahead. I could hear the music, and smell the food, and see the midway. Already, there were people everywhere, crowding around the dunking tank and the goldfish game and the ring-a-bottle-of-Coke stand.

"Do you have money for cotton candy, Wheezie?" asked Roscoe, drool oozing from the corners of his mouth.

"No," I said, "that's why we need to find a job."

"Why?" asked Roscoe.

"To make money, Roscoe," I snapped. "To buy food. To live."

"How wong are we running away for?" Roscoe asked, gawking up at the Ferris wheel.

"As long as it takes," I said, "for Mama and Daddy to get back together. Could be three days. Could be three weeks. Could be three years."

"Three years?" stammered Roscoe, tripping over a cord leading to the merry-go-round. "That's too wong, Wheezie."

I ignored him, marching up to the operator of the ride.

"Excuse me, sir," I said, "are you the owner?"

The man nodded, grumpy and slow.

"Well," I said, clearing my throat, "my name is Mildred and this is my brother Myron."

"*Mildred,*" Roscoe said behind me, kicking my ankle.

"Stop it, Myron," I said. "Don't mind him," I told the man. "He's a bit slow." Roscoe kicked me again and I continued.

"We're looking for a job, sir," I said, as the carousel horses circled past. "We're orphans, you see, since our daddy died in Vietnam." Roscoe sniffled, then booted me again.

"Do you need any help?" I asked. "We're willing to travel: town to town to town, all over America."

"All over *America?*" Roscoe shouted, and I kicked him.

The man stared, his face still grumpy. "Don't need no help," he said.

"You don't know what you're missing," I called as we walked away. "We work hard and cheap." Dust swirled as the breeze picked up and I sneezed.

"Wheezie," said Roscoe, "why'd you say that stuff about Vietnam?"

I shrugged. "I guess it was on my mind," I replied, sneezing again.

"Is the Vietnam War still happening, now that Uncle Ob died?" Roscoe asked as we passed the cotton-candy stand. A man was whirling pink sugar around cones, smiling and singing. I stopped.

"Roscoe," I said, "just because one guy dies, doesn't mean that war is no more. Just like divorce. There've been zillions of kids hurt by it, but it still goes on and on and on."

"Oh," said Roscoe, looking down at the ground.

"Stay here," I said. "I'm going to get us a job."

Striding up to the man behind the stand, I put on my best smile and smoothed down my hair. "Excuse me, sir," I said, leaning on the counter, "do you need any help?"

The man chuckled. "I need lots of help, sweetie," he said, "but I don't make enough money to pay for it." The cotton candy spun and my mouth watered as I swallowed hard.

"Do you know if anybody around here needs any workers?" I asked.

"I don't know, sugar," said the man with a smile.

"Maybe this wasn't a very good idea,

Wheezie," Roscoe commented as I trudged toward him.

"Wheezie is always right," I whimpered, plodding across the midway, already tired of running away.

Chapter Twenty-four

Zebedee Blessing

The dunking tank didn't need help. The goldfish game didn't need help. The ring-a-bottle-of-Coke stand didn't need help, and neither did the french fry place or the bumper cars. I was beginning to think that the only people who needed help were Roscoe and me.

"There's one more place we can try," I said, leading the way. "The moon walk."

"Hooray!" Roscoe hollered, clapping his hands. "I want to walk on the moon!"

Roscoe and Buford and I stood and gazed at the moon walk. It loomed like a huge balloon, bulging and billowing and bouncing with jumping kids.

I closed my eyes and whispered. *Please. This is our last chance. Please let us get a job. Please, please, please.*

When I opened my eyes, an old man was slowly unzipping the moon-walk exit. Kids poured jabbering from inside, streaming every which way into the midway, and the man turned.

"Wow," said Roscoe, "he's *old!*"

The man had a face like an ancient potato, all wizened and brown, with knots for eyes. His nose was broad and flared, and he had ears like jug handles, topped off with a shock of white hair as curly as Luna's wool.

Roscoe and I stopped and stared as Buford bolted toward the man, leaped up, and licked his hand.

"Buford acts like he knows him," I whispered.

The man's hands, twisted like the trunks of old trees, reached for Buford as a smile crinkled across his brown face. Buford licked him again, and the man looked up at Roscoe and me, skin sagging and swinging from his chin.

"This puppy belong to you younguns?"

he said, in a voice weak and shaky and gray, like old cigar smoke.

Roscoe and I nodded, two dummies on the same string.

"What's his name?" asked the man, his lips puckered and thin. He didn't seem to have any teeth.

"Buford," Roscoe stuttered. "His name is Buford, but sometimes I call him Wassie because he's so smart."

The man laughed, a dry-chicken cackle that rasped from his withered lips.

"I like that," he said. "A youngun of invention. Most children nowadays lack imagination, what with too much television and all. What's your name, son?"

Roscoe blinked, then chomped on his lip. "Roscoe," he said. "Roscoe Byler."

I elbowed him. "His real name is Myron, sir," I said. "Roscoe is just a nickname."

The man nodded, his chin skin swaying. "And your name, young lady?" he asked, fixing those knot eyes hard and steady on mine.

"Mildred," I blurted. "Mildred Clampett."

The man chortled. "Just like 'The Beverly Hillbillies,' eh? I think the world of that program."

"Me, too," blubbered Roscoe. "Do you wike 'The Price Is Right'?"

"Wouldn't miss it," said the man, slapping a gnarled hand against his leg.

Hiss, gasp, snuffle. Hiss, gasp, snuffle. Hiss, gasp, snuffle, wheeze, snort, chortle. Roscoe and the man sounded as though they were made for each other, cracking up together like the oldest of buddies.

"My name," said the old man (*wheeze, gasp, snort*), "is" (*snuffle, snort, chortle*) "Zebedee. Zebedee Blessing."

"Is that your real name?" Roscoe asked, dull eyes wide.

"Real as the mole on my nose," said the old man, draping a wrinkled brown arm around Roscoe.

"Are you the owner of the moon walk?" I asked, and Zebedee nodded.

"Since 1945," he said. "Bought it soon's I came home from World War Two."

"You were in a *war*?" Roscoe asked, jaw dropping. "And you didn't get killed?"

The man looked down at himself, then up at Roscoe. "Not that I know of," he said, and he and Roscoe went at it again. *Hiss, gasp, snuffle. Hiss, gasp, snuffle. Hiss, gasp, snuffle, snort, chortle.*

When they finally stopped, Roscoe looked Zebedee dead in the eyes. "We need a job," he said. "Could you use some help with the moon wawk?"

"Myron," said Zebedee, "I need help like I need a new set of teeth." He licked his lips, slow, purple tongue swollen and slobbery.

"We'd be good at working here," Roscoe said. "We watched the moon wawk on TV. And I made a space machine, because some-day I'm going to walk on the moon." He toed the dust, suddenly shy. "Buford and me will be the first boy and dog in space," he said, ears red.

Zebedee nodded, looking at Roscoe as if he were the most brilliant thing this side of the sun.

"And why might a young fella like you be in need of a job, Myron?" Zebedee asked.

"We need to make money to buy food," spluttered Roscoe. "So we can eat."

Zebedee's knot eyes softened, like a potato in the oven.

"Where are your folks?" he asked.

I cleared my throat and crossed my fingers behind my back. "Passed on, sir. Myron and I are orphans, on our own for the past six months."

"Orphans?" Zebedee blinked hard. "With no family to call your own?"

"That's right, sir," I said.

Zebedee raised his eyes to the sky, shaking his head. "My lands!" he said. "The answer to our prayer!"

I looked at Roscoe and he looked at me, and we both looked at Zebedee.

"My wife, Beulah, and I been prayin' for younguns for nigh on fifty years!" said Zebedee. "Ever since we lost our little one, we been askin' for children to care for, to be a family. And now, here ya are!"

Zebedee turned toward a tiny white trailer parked behind the moon walk. "Beulah!" he hollered. "Beulah, honey, come quick! The Lord done sent us our younguns!"

I gawked at Roscoe, he gawked at me, and then we both gawked at the door of the trailer slowly swinging open.

Chapter Twenty-five

At Least a Million Years Old

Beulah must have been at least a million years old, with a face like antique paper, all crinkly and yellow. She had eyes as pale as the moon, with blue circles beneath, and a tiny fluff of hair wispy-light like white cotton candy. She wore a faded flowered dress and a look of surprise, as if she'd just swallowed a snow cone whole.

"Zebedee," she said, in a soft voice all full of scratches like an old record, "did you say these younguns are to be ours?"

Zebedee nodded, and she clasped her wrinkled, blue-veined hands together, the door swinging closed behind her. "Oh, my stars," she said. And then she burst into sobs, gentle spells of crying that reminded me of rain on the roof. "My stars," she kept saying over and over like a broken record.

I looked at Roscoe and he looked at me, as Zebedee limped to the woman and gathered her skinny old body into a shaky hug. "Now, honey," he said, "we always knew the Lord would send 'em someday. Well, someday is today."

"See what you got us into?" I whispered to Roscoe. "These two are nutty as a fruit-cake."

"Not me," slobbered Roscoe. "It was your idea to run away, Wheezie."

"Wheezie is always right," I said, trying to convince myself as much as Roscoe. Buford waddled through the dust and up to Beulah, sniffing her scrawny legs.

"Come in, children," called Beulah. "I was just cooking some dinner." She opened the trailer door, and a wonderful smell wafted out. My stomach growled.

"Well," I said, "maybe just for a little while."

Zebedee limped to the moon walk and

hung a sign on the entrance. "Closin' for a spell," he yelled to some kids who clutched tickets on the midway. "Need time to get to know our new family."

Roscoe sniffled. "I don't want to be their kids, Wheezie," he blubbered in my ear.

"Roscoe," I hissed, "don't be so dumb. We'll just have some food, help out with the moon walk, and stay for the night. We need a place to sleep, don't we?"

Roscoe nodded, nose red and dripping. "I miss Ma and Pap," he said.

And I miss Mama and Daddy.

"What will we do tomorrow, Wheezie?" asked Roscoe as Zebedee hobbled to the trailer.

I thought for a minute. "Run away again," I said with a shrug. "Don't worry so much, Roscoe. I have a plan."

"I hate your pwans," Roscoe wailed as Zebedee opened the trailer door and Buford scooted inside.

"Stifle," I hissed, fixing my eyes upon that tiny white trailer and my stomach upon the meal waiting inside. I kicked Roscoe's ankle, then led the way to the door.

Beulah was standing before a miniature red stove, stirring something hot and steaming. Zebedee leaned over and peered inside a little refrigerator.

"Like Coca-Cola, Mildred?" he asked, and I nodded.

"Ma says Coca-Cowa makes me jittery," Roscoe whined, plucking at his elbow.

"Myron," I said, booting him, "Ma *used* to say that. She's gone now, remember?" I shot Roscoe a glare.

Beulah turned, beaming. "I just can't believe that we're going to be your folks," she said.

"Me, neither," I mumbled. *What have we gotten into?* I was thinking. These people were as crazy as they were old.

"Hope you two like to travel," Zebedee said, toting a bottle of Coke to the small table. "We gallivant all over creation, town-to-town-to-town, just a-hightailin' it to every fair we can find. Why, we leave tomorrow for Jersey." He deposited the soda bottle on the table and rummaged in a cupboard as Buford settled himself beneath the table.

"Jersey?" I asked. "You mean *New* Jersey?" I sunk into a chair, my heart pounding.

"The one and only," Zebedee said, producing a handful of paper plates and napkins. "Why, you two will get an education, what with all the tourin' around we do. Course we'll have to do some schoolin', too, ya know." He fixed me with those knot eyes, setting the table with a circle of red-checked plates.

"Um . . . Mister Zebedee, sir," I stammered, not quite knowing how to break the news, "all we really need is a place to stay the night. You see, there's a family just waiting to adopt us, and come tomorrow everything will be final."

Zebedee's face fell, his chin skin swaying lower. "You mean that you and Myron won't be our younguns after all?" he asked, running a gnarled hand through his fuzzy white hair. Beulah had stopped stirring, and now she was staring, pale eyes wide.

"Um . . . no, sir, I'm sorry, sir," I stuttered. "We'd really *like* to be your kids, though," I added, nudging Roscoe.

"Maybe you could be kind of like our grandparents. Our adopted grandparents, whenever you're in the area." I was babbling, and beginning to sound like Roscoe.

"And we'd just love to eat with you and Beulah, sir, and we sure do plan to help you with the moon walk all night long until you close it up. We work hard . . ." My stomach growled, loud, as Beulah walked slow and shaky with a pan of spaghetti.

"It's all right, dear," she said, sitting the steaming pan on a hotpad and patting my hand. "I was a tad bit worried that perhaps Zebedee and I are too outdated for children, anyway."

I nodded, taking a deep breath and looking at these two people who were at least a million years old. Zebedee was ladling mounds of spaghetti onto my plate, and Beulah was rooting in a cupboard.

"Some folks have younguns and some don't," said Zebedee, shaking his head as he piled a mountain of spaghetti before Roscoe and his drooling mouth. "And some younguns have folks and some don't." He shuffled over to Beulah and draped a wrinkled brown arm over her skinny shoulders, planting a smooch on her crinkly-paper cheek.

"And those who do," he said, "best realize how doggone lucky they are, and stay together forever the way it was meant to be."

I nodded, thinking how these million-year-old people had a lot of horse sense, and then I dug into my spaghetti, feeling as if I hadn't eaten in a hundred years.

Chapter Twenty-six

Nothing Left in the World

The wagon was gone. Angry tears crept down my cheeks as I stood in the moonlit dark and stared at the rope dragging from the hitch of the tractor and leading to nowhere. I sank to my knees and wept, feeling as if I had nothing left in the world. No change of clothing, no pillow, no toothbrush, no soap. Not a thing to call my own but the dirty clothes on my back, a mood ring that wouldn't turn green, and a copper bracelet with the name of a dead man on it. I cried and cried, feeling empty as the crumpled french fry cones littering the ground around me, thinking of every sad thing in my life until the tears finally dried and the sobbing stopped. I struggled to my feet and wiped my eyes, looking out at the fading lights of the Grace County Fair.

It was past midnight and the fair was closing, the rides silent and dark. I took a big breath and started to walk, aching all over from helping with the moon walk. I never knew a job could be so much hard work.

"Please, Mama and Daddy," I said out loud, "please find me soon, so that I can go home." *And we'll stay together. Together, forever, because I never want to run away again.*

I hurried past the dunking tank and the goldfish game and the ring-a-bottle-of-Coke stand, the french fry place and the cotton-candy stand and the merry-go-round and the Ferris wheel. I couldn't believe things that were so much fun were so spooky at night, all silhouetted and silent, waiting for people to liven them up. Gazing at the merry-go-round, I could have sworn I saw it move, the painted horses gliding up and down and around, quiet and slow. I blinked hard, and they were still.

Heart racing, I started to run. I couldn't

wait to be inside the trailer with Roscoe and Buford and Beulah and Zebedee, safe and away from the night. Pillow or no pillow, sleeping bag or not, I knew I'd sleep sound tonight.

Making a break for it, I bolted for the little white trailer, my heart hammering so loud that I could hear it in my ears. And then I heard something else: a wheeze, coming from deep inside my chest. Asthma.

My chest got tighter and the wheezing louder, as I started to cough. I coughed and coughed and coughed, hacking and gasping, as the pounding grew louder and louder.

As I stumbled closer to the trailer, I realized that the thumping sound wasn't my heart . . . it was Roscoe. Jumping up and down, up and down, he leaped around and around the moon walk, arms flying at his sides and Buford bouncing at his feet.

"The *Eagle* has wanded!" he hollered, flying like a bird through the air inside the moon walk.

"Roscoe," I gasped, collapsing at the entrance, "help."

Chapter Twenty-seven

Wishing with All My Heart to Be Able to Breathe

"Didn't you bring your breather thing, Wheezie?" asked Roscoe, and I shook my head.

"Forgot . . . it," I choked, wishing with all my heart to be able to breathe.

"What's wrong with Mildred?" It was Zebedee, hunched in the trailer door.

"She has asthma," Roscoe announced, panting and dripping sweat.

"Asthma!" declared Zebedee. "Why, my lands, a soul could die of that!"

Roscoe drew a ragged breath, then lit off into the night as if he'd been shot from a cannon. "Don't worry, Wheezie!" he hol-

155

lered, his voice fading away in the dark. "I won't wet you die. Never, ever, ever in a million years."

I began to cry, choking and heaving.

Roscoe reappeared. "Do you have a tewe-phone?" he asked Zebedee.

"No, Myron, we sure don't," said Zebe-dee, and Roscoe took off again.

"Doctor Mack lives just on the other side of the woods, Wheezie," he hollered. "I know how to get there." I heard a lip-smacking sound, and Buford waddled off. "Wassie will help," Roscoe called, and then a hush settled like dust.

"That Myron," said Zebedee, shaking his head in the doorway, "calling you Wheezie on account of your breathing. What a sense of humor that boy has. Even in a time of trouble, he still tries to lighten things up for his sister. That Myron sure is a card."

I kept on crying, sobbing and choking and heaving and gasping.

"I . . . hate . . . asthma," I huffed, stomp-ing my heels in the dirt.

"Now, Mildred," said Zebedee, hobbling through the dark. "It doesn't do any good to get mad about that which we can't help. Anger just poisons the heart." He bent down and gently lifted me into his arms, staggering slowly toward the trailer.

"Now," he said, depositing me onto a tiny green couch, "you must relax a spell. That big brother of yours will fetch you some help in two shakes of a lamb's tail. You sure are a lucky gal, Mildred, to have a brother like that."

I nodded, propped against the arm of the sofa and gasping, as Beulah hovered over me and Zebedee sank heavily into a torn armchair and switched on a tiny television set.

"A tad bit of television will take your mind off what ails ya, Mildred," he said.

I nodded again, trying to relax and fighting to breathe, as Beulah eyed me anxiously from above.

"Durn shame it's not time for 'The Price Is Right,'" said Zebedee. "We could guess prices."

I nodded, coughing and coughing.

"How old are you, Mildred?" asked Beulah, and I held up ten fingers, then two.

"Twelve!" said Beulah. "Why, you're nigh on a woman, Mildred. I remember when I was a young gal of twelve . . ."

Beulah perched on the edge of the sofa and launched into a story that went on and on, all about the Great Depression and World War II and food rationing and flour-sack dresses.

"You younguns nowadays have it easy," Zebedee said, running a hand through his crop of curly hair. "You think *you* have problems . . ."

A news bulletin flashed across the television screen, and I caught my breath, the little bit of it I had left. Roscoe and I were on TV, our school pictures from last year lined up side by side like partners in crime. "Two children are missing in Grace County tonight," said the announcer, and I cast a sideways look at Zebedee. He was sitting straight up in his chair, gazing at the television set with his toothless mouth hanging open and his chin swinging.

"Mildred," he said, "is that Myron and you?"

Before I could answer, Roscoe burst

through the door, Buford and The Barn Owl tottering behind.

"Wheezie," Roscoe blurted, "there are powice officers all over the pwace, and one of them has our wagon."

Chapter Twenty-eight

Brand-New Day, Same Old Problems

It was sometime between night and day when Mama and Daddy stormed through the door.

"Louise Olivia Moore," growled Daddy, eyes bloodshot and puffy beneath a red bandanna tied around his head, "just what did you think you were doing . . ."

"Running away," said Mama, finishing his sentence the way she used to do.

I sighed and closed my eyes, tired of questions. After all the police and their zillions of questions, I just plumb ran out of answers.

"Young lady," said Daddy, softer-voiced now, "you had us worried . . ."

"Sick," said Mama. "Just worried sick."

I slowly pried open my eyes, looking up at my parents from the tiny sofa.

"Sorry," I squeaked, gritting my teeth into a smile.

Zebedee and Roscoe came in the door, followed by Beulah and Buford and The Barn Owl and Evie Nettle, then Aunt Ida and Uncle Ollie. They huddled in a little group by the open door, pretending to make small talk among themselves as we continued our conversation. Evie Nettle was sneaking peeks at me in between words, I could see.

"What time is it?" I asked, yawning.

Daddy took a deep breath. "Time for you . . ."

"To face the truth," said Mama, and they looked at each other and smiled. Really smiled, for the first time in ages. My heart leaped and I reached out my arms.

"I love you both," I said, and they bent down and drew me tight into a six-armed bear hug, the way we always used to do.

"And we both love you," said Daddy, tears plopping from his cheeks. Mama began to cry, too, and then me.

"I'm sorry," I said. "I just thought that if you two realized how you'd feel if something happened to me, then maybe you wouldn't get a divorce."

Mama drew a sharp breath, and Daddy pulled back.

Roscoe stumbled across the room. "And I only ran away because I didn't want to go to Ob's funeral," he announced, then bumbled back to the group at the door. "And Wheezie *made* me run away, too," he called as Evie Nettle gawked and The Barn Owl fiddled with his stethoscope.

"Wheezie," said Mama, her long hair falling across my cheek, "if we get a divorce, it has nothing to do with *you*."

"It has *everything* to do with me," I shouted, and they all stared, blue eyes and pale-moon eyes and knot eyes and beady black eyes goggling.

Uncle Ollie motioned the group outside, and I waited until the door banged shut.

"It has everything to do with me," I said again, quiet. "I'm a combination of both of you, right?"

Mama and Daddy nodded, standing farther apart now.

"So," I said, "if you two divorce, you tear me in two. Rip me apart. Divide me in half like a candy bar or something."

Mama and Daddy didn't answer, so I went on.

"What are you doing here *together*, if you're still thinking about divorce?" I demanded, waving my hand at them. My mood ring was red, my chest tight, and my heart hurting.

"We both . . ." said Daddy.

"Love you," Mama said.

I rubbed my eyes, then sighed. "And I love both of you," I said again. I shook my head, frustrated and exhausted. "I'm too tired to fight anymore," I said.

"And that's exactly how we feel," said Mama. "Too tired to fight anymore."

I looked from one to the other, fear clenching my throat. "So what are you saying?" I asked. "You're getting a divorce, for sure?"

"A separation, honey," Daddy said, soft and sad. "I've signed a six-month lease on a farm, and you'll visit me every weekend. When the six months are up . . . well, then we'll see how it's going and make a final decision."

"Holy moley," I said, sinking back into the saggy sofa, "a *farm*. Does it have animals?"

"Not yet," Daddy said with a smile.

I had an idea. "Daddy," I said, "if it's okay with Uncle Ollie and Aunt Ida, could I bring a lamb? Her name is Luna."

Daddy shrugged. "Every farm girl needs a pet," he said, and I smiled.

Mama sighed, rubbing her eyes. "We need to be going, Wheezie. There's lots to do for the . . ."

She paused, taking big breaths. "For the funeral," she said, eyes filling with tears.

Mama stepped outside, then Daddy, then me. The sun was rising, breaking like a cracked egg over the moon walk, and the sky was pale blue and streaking with pink. *Brand-new day, same old problems*, I thought, looking around as the Grace County Annual Fair was packed into trucks and trailers, leaving for another year. *And I'm staying here.* Running away hadn't gotten me anywhere.

And then I saw them, within the moon walk and jumping like a bunch of idiots: Roscoe and The Barn Owl and Evie Nettle and

Uncle Ollie and Aunt Ida, all leaping circles around Buford, bouncing him up and down, up and down, like some four-legged fur ball of a circus clown.

"Wassie has wanded!" Roscoe hollered, as Buford wiggled his stub of a tail and The Barn Owl's stethoscope flew up and down, smacking him in the forehead.

"Come on in, Wheezie," Aunt Ida yelled, holding her glasses to her nose as she jumped.

"We're walkin' on the moon!" rasped Uncle Ollie, limping after Aunt Ida.

"We're havin' a high time, Mildred," said Zebedee, chin swinging as he took tiny, old-man steps around the edge of the moon walk, grasping Beulah's hand. "Pumps up the circulation: good for what ails ya."

I watched them, smiling in spite of myself.

"How's your breathing, Wheezie?" shouted The Barn Owl, peering out through the mesh sides.

"Great," I said, taking a long and slow breath. The morning smelled good, and so did the new perfume Mama was wearing.

The sunshine was warm, the breeze cool, the sky blue. Daddy put his arm around me, drawing me close.

"Everything will work out, Wheezie," he said.

"And we'll all be much happier," Mama chimed in.

I looked up at the brand-new day, then down at my same old parents, who were waiting for my reply.

"*We'll see*," I said.

Chapter Twenty-nine

Bidding Ob Good-bye

I sat between Mama and Daddy in the front pew of Grace E.C. Church, staring at the flowers and the preacher and the candles, trying not to look at Ob, so pale and still in a silk-lined box.

The preacher rambled on and on, talking of how the United States could be proud of Ob for giving up his life. *Ob didn't give up his life*, I thought. Something *stole* Ob's life, something called war that I didn't understand any more than I understood divorce. Mama sniffled at my side, and I touched her hand, then Daddy's, glad to be in the middle of my parents without a fight going on.

Allowing my eyes to slide toward Ob, I looked first at his hands, folded and white, and then at his face. The face scared me: it was fat and ashy and fake, layered with makeup thick and white as paste. It was *somebody else*'s face, not Ob's. *Ob*'s face was tanned and smooth and full of movement and life, with eyes like sky and a smile like sunshine. I looked away.

The stench of flowers was making me sick. Flowers and perfume and candles and hair spray—the odors whipped through the church by the whirl of the ceiling fans overhead. No wonder Roscoe wasn't here.

Twisting the copper band on my wrist, I focused on the preacher. Mama reached over and touched the bracelet, resting her pink-nailed finger gently on the etched letters, then catching my eye. She couldn't decide whether to smile or cry, I could tell by the wet shine in her eyes and the twitch of her mouth.

"Ob was a good guy," she whispered in my ear, and I nodded, my heart catching as I thought of how Mama was my age when

Ob was born. I knew how *I'd* love a baby brother, just love him to death.

And now the preacher was talking about Ob being a good guy, one who played a mean game of baseball and loved his family something fierce. He told of how he sang in the choir and earned pins for perfect attendance in Sunday school and rang the bell on Sunday mornings when he was just knee-high to a grasshopper. He told of how Granny and Gramps went to Grace E.C., raising Ollie and Ob and Mama in the church. He told of how Ob slept right through his christening as a baby, just lay there in his white blanket and slept as sweet as sugar while water sprinkled across his little face.

The preacher told of all these things, but he didn't tell of eyes blue like sky or a smile like sunshine or a redbird feather in his pocket. He didn't tell of how Ob felt to hug: all skinny and strong and full of spunk. He didn't tell of how Ob planted a tree for me or how he swung me in circles in the air around him when I was little. He didn't tell of how long it would be until we'd see him again.

Mama passed me a tissue and I shredded it to confetti, dropping the pieces in my lap. My mood ring was the craziest mix of colors I'd ever seen: slashes of red and black and orange and pink, with blue streaked everywhere in between, but no green. I turned it until the stone faced backward, clenching it tight in my palm.

Organ music bellowed melancholy through the church, and the candles flickered as a breeze wafted through the screens. The flowers were everywhere, all shades of the rainbow and blazing bright. I squeezed shut my eyes, then opened them as people began to file past the casket, bidding Ob good-bye.

Ollie and Ida and Mama and Daddy and I waited until everybody was gone and only we were left. Us and Ob and the preacher and God. I took a deep breath and stood, smoothing my dress and fussing with my hair and picking at my fingernails. Ollie and Ida went first, then Daddy, then Mama and me. Mama bent low over the casket, kissing Ob's cheek and stroking his hand, whispering softly as I pretended to read the little cards budding within the bouquets of flowers.

There was a flag, an American flag, folded at Ob's feet. Red, white, and blue, the colors Ob fought and died for. I reached out and touched the stars, silky and white like the stuff shining on all sides of Ob's body.

"Your turn, Wheezie," Mama whispered, and I moved forward, a lump in my throat. I looked at the flowers and I looked at the candles and I looked at the photograph of Ob as a boy. In the casket beside Ob's body were his fishing rod and his baseball glove and some medals from the war. And something red, hiding behind Ob's shoulder. I reached out and it was the redbird feather, tucked with the card beneath Ob's arm. *This feather is for good luck in the Vietnam War. It's from a redbird who flew from the tree you planted for me when I was born. Use it to fly away from Vietnam and back home again, when the war gets too bad to stand.* I started to cry and couldn't stop, tears plopping onto Ob.

"Good-bye, Ob," I sobbed, bending fast to brush a kiss across his cheek. "I love you."

I turned away, something ripping deep

within, and then I saw them: Roscoe and Buford, walking side by side down the aisle, coming to say their good-byes to Uncle Ob. I stopped and watched as Roscoe lifted Buford into his arms and held him to the casket, waving his paw in a final farewell.

Chapter Thirty

Somewhere behind the Moon

The moon glowed full and bright, round and white like the pearl earrings Mama wore for Ob's funeral.

"Do you believe that Ob is up there behind the moon somewhere?" I asked Roscoe as we sprawled flat on our backs in the grass.

"Somewhere," said Roscoe. He gazed at the sky for a while, then turned to me. "Do you think animals go to heaven?" he asked.

"Sure," I said. "Ob is most likely up there taking care of the White Giant and Bacon Lady and that beagle dog he had when he was little."

Roscoe grinned, then nodded. "Ob would wike that," he said.

We turned back to the sky and were silent for a while. I took a deep breath, smelling lilacs and ripe tomatoes and the end of summer.

"Do you know what I named this summer, Roscoe?" I asked as Buford waddled across the yard and plopped down between us.

Roscoe shook his head, still staring at the moon and the stars and the sky.

"The Summer of the Great Divide," I said, patting Buford's head.

"Why?" asked Roscoe.

"Well," I said, "there was a lot of dividing going on. My parents made a Great Divide when they sent me here to Grace, so far from home. I was divided from them and they were divided from me as they decided whether to divide from each other."

"Are they getting a divorce for sure?" asked Roscoe.

I shrugged. "Who knows?" I said. "Only the good Lord and the lawyers. And, as Zebedee says, it does no good to get mad about things we can't help. Just poisons the heart."

I smiled and went on. "During this summer," I said, "I saw division between animals and people, between people and people, and between you and me. I guess you could say you and I were at war, in a way."

Roscoe looked at me, teeth flashing in the night.

"But I guess you could also say that we've made peace, seeing as how you helped save my life, twice." Buford licked my hand, and I pulled him close. "You and I have made peace, Buford and I have made peace, and we've made peace with Evie Nettle, even though she was the one who called the police."

Roscoe nodded. "And you're not so mean as you used to be, Wheezie."

"I know," I said. "I decided life is too short to waste time being mean." I stared at the sky, a black curtain dividing here from there. "Uncle Ob's death made me decide that," I said.

Roscoe rubbed his eyes.

"Ob was only nineteen," I said, "at the end of being a teenager. And now here we are at the beginning." I sighed. "That's another divide: this summer was the division between being kids and growing up. And I guess we're growing up."

"I guess," said Roscoe, and laughed. *Hiss, gasp, snuffle.* "I don't really want to grow up."

"I do," I said. "I want to walk on the moon."

"Wheezie," Roscoe said, sitting up and clapping, "I have a surprise!" He stood, grasping my hands and pulling me up. "Follow me," he said.

I did, through the yard and up the trail and to the dump, where Roscoe's space machine gleamed. Glittering silver in the light of the moon, the outhouse shone once more, shimmering even brighter than before.

"Pap bought me a whole roll of *new* tinfoil," Roscoe said, proud. He flung open the door. "Come inside," he said, and flicked on a flashlight hung from the ceiling.

I stepped in and saw that the walls were covered with feathers: chicken feathers and duck feathers and sparrow feathers and barn-swallow feathers. There were robin feathers and crow feathers and blackbird feathers and turkey-buzzard feathers. And there was one redbird feather, stuck alone in a crack of wood between the seats.

"The feathers will help me fwy to the moon," said Roscoe, throwing out his arms and flapping them. "The *Eagle* has wanded!" he shouted.

And then he plucked the redbird feather from the wood and presented it to me with a bow.

"For good wuck in school this year," he said. "Use it to fwy back here if home gets too bad to stand."

I stroked the soft tufts of the feather, my eyes brimming full with tears and my ring shining green in the gleam of the flashlight.

"Thank you, Roscoe," I said. "I'll keep it for always."

We stepped outside and saw light, sweeping the trees and glowing bright in the drive.

"It's time to go home," I said.

I gave Roscoe a quick hug, stuck the feather in my pocket, and lit off through the dark, running for the light.